# Falling for a Bossy Cowboy

## VARGAS RANCH BOOK 3

## Karen Baney

desert life
media

Falling for a Bossy Cowboy: Vargas Ranch Book 3
By Karen Baney

Publisher:
Desert Life Media, LLC
Gilbert, AZ 85295

www.karenbaney.com

Printed in the United States of America

ISBN 978-1-960217-16-5

*With regard to the works of man,*
*by the word of your lips*
*I have avoided the ways of the violent.*
*My steps have held fast to your paths;*
*my feet have not slipped.*

Psalms 17:4-5

# 1

MADISON MOORE PUSHED through the pain. It wasn't the first time, nor would it be the last. A guttural "ha" escaped her lips as she extended her arm and leaned low to send the tennis ball back across the net. Fire spread through her right shoulder. She winced as she prepared to backhand the ball. She squelched a smile at the soft thud of the sphere bouncing off her racket netting, as it sailed toward a hard-to-reach corner of the opposite side of the court.

The warm sun beat down on her tanned arms. Madison had always enjoyed playing in Arizona in the winter. It didn't feel like the Januaries she had grown up with in Colorado.

"Ha!" she grunted with her next hit.

"Hey!" Bella Gaines, her sparring partner, complained. "Watch the legs!"

Madison's lips tilted up in a half-smile when Bella volleyed the bright yellow ball over the net. It flew just out of reach, so Madison leaned to smack it back. The pain seared through her shoulder, causing her to drop her racket. Her left arm crossed over her chest as her hand locked onto her hurting shoulder.

"Enough for today," Coach Layla said. "Best put ice on it."

Madison frowned as her personal assistant Sydney retrieved her racket. Seemed Syd had been doing that a lot lately—ever since the surgery.

Worry threaded around Madison's heart for the hundredth time. In two months, she needed to be ready for a huge charity tournament in Phoenix. If she didn't compete in it or did poorly, it might be the end of her career. She was still young. Twenty-six. Many players continued in the sport well into their thirties, especially if they were top tier, like she was.

As she silently walked toward the locker room, long ponytail bouncing against her back, the life-changing injury flashed in her mind's eye. September in New York City. The US Open. Just like her last hit this morning, Madison overextended her arm to return the ball and avoid points awarded to her opponent. She felt the tear the second it happened, crumpling to the hard court surface. Her boyfriend, also her personal trainer, rushed the court and carried her off. International TV cameras captured the whole thing.

It had been the last day of the Open. She was in the number one spot for Women's Singles. By forfeiting her last match, she lost her chance at winning. One match away from a Grand Slam—winning all four major world tournaments. It would have been her second year in a row.

Instead, her manager had rushed her to the hospital. The next day her lame boyfriend dumped her by text message. Funny how he befriended the winner that day, confirming he had only dated her to further his own career. Scum.

As Madison entered the locker room, Syd followed behind her. She must have sensed Madison's mood because she quickly packed up Madison's equipment and lugged it out to the rented SUV.

Madison showered and changed into shorts and a ruffled short-sleeved top. She donned a pair of fancy flip-flops, showing off her perfect pedicure. She may feel terrible, but she looked great.

"Where is this place again?" Madison asked as she

tossed her gym bag into the back of the SUV. Then she climbed into the back seat behind the driver, her manager, Kevin.

"Vargas Guest Ranch & Resort is in Wickenburg. About two and a half hours due west," Syd replied.

"Guest ranch? They have pro-grade tennis courts?"

Kevin grunted. "Yes. Like I'd let you rehab anywhere substandard."

"But, a guest ranch?"

"They have a state-of-the-art sports complex that just opened. Our buddy Cole Gregory works there now."

"Not my buddy. Yours, if I recall."

Kevin's eyes flicked to the rearview mirror. "You have a problem with him?"

"Nope."

If Madison remembered the sports agent, she had absolutely no problem with him. He was easy on the eyes and she even nursed a bit of a crush on him a few years ago. He had never seemed interested in her. Rumor had it he was religious. Never dated clients or potential clients or friends of clients. The guy had a reputation of being aboveboard. Always.

When Kevin's gaze returned to the road, Madison watched the cars zip by on the eight-lane highway. The throbbing in her shoulder had subsided after icing it for the first twenty minutes of the drive. As the city gave way to open desert, she remembered what Mom said when she FaceTime'd with her earlier in the week.

*Consider the ravens: they neither sow nor reap, they have neither storehouse nor barn, and yet God feeds them. Of how much more value are you than the birds!*

Mom often interjected Bible verses into their conversations. Verses Madison had grown up memorizing, like that one from Luke 12. The faith she had abandoned when fame and glory lured her into believing the lie that she had created her success on her own. One torn shoulder muscle, hours of surgery, and months of rehab had humbled her.

*Father God, You are enough. Thank you for reminding me I am in Your hands. Whether I play pro tennis again.*

The tension coiled around her shoulders, causing the throbbing to return. Madison really hoped God might let her continue to play tennis. It was the only thing she knew. She had never considered what life would look like after tennis.

Madison sighed and popped in her earbuds for the rest of the drive, listening to worship music to comfort her soul. She didn't want to go back to a life far from God. She smiled. Guess that sort of made her religious, too.

DERIN VARGAS FROWNED at the ridiculous polo shirt. A man built like him wasn't meant to wear such a shirt. The collar looked too small even as it gaped open. He unbuttoned the last button. Still didn't look right. He tugged at the opening. Then he ran a finger under each cuff, stretching out the sleeves. The soft fabric felt comfortable. It was the collar and short-sleeves that had him in a surly mood. That and khakis.

"Are you sure I have to dress like this?" he asked as he stepped out of his bedroom and into the living room.

Cole Gregory entered from his bedroom on the other side of the living room. His eyes traveled from Derin's cowboy boots to the stiff pants and up to the shirt. A chuckle echoed in the room as Cole's face broke into a huge grin.

"Don't think cowboy boots are the right footwear."

Derin shook his head and crossed his arms over his broad chest, glaring at his new roommate. "I draw the line at that."

Cole leaned against the doorframe of his room. What

had Derin been thinking to let his friend room with him in his temporary home? Oh, yeah. Accountability. That was it.

"Maybe we should get you some button-down executive shirts with the logo. What about your dark jeans? How's the polo look with them?"

Derin toed off his two-tone brown boots before heading back into his room. He was twenty-nine, for goodness's sake. He ought to be able to dress himself. Add that to the long list of things he felt unprepared to do. Dalton must not be thinking straight to put Derin in charge of the sports complex and rehab center. Sure, he loved sports. Was downright excited that a famous pro tennis player would arrive in a few hours. But Derin was a cowboy through and through. Ranch foreman suited him better than, well, this new job and the clothes that came with it.

After he donned his black jeans and swapped to a black belt with a large silver buckle, he stepped into the living room again. The aroma of freshly brewed coffee filled the air.

"Hmm," Cole murmured from near the coffeepot. "You wearing your Stetson?"

"Duh?"

Cole snickered. "Here, you need some coffee."

"So, is this good enough?"

"It'll have to do. 'Cause no way are you meeting Madison Moore in a checkered shirt."

Derin swallowed hard. No one had told him the pro tennis player was a woman. Or that she was Madison Moore—only one of the most drop-dead gorgeous athletes in the country. He admired her skill, too. She had almost swept the worldwide women's single tournaments two years in a row.

Yeah, so, tennis. His brothers gave him grief about his love of tennis. To quote Devon, "No self-respecting cowboy follows tennis." Except Derin. Derin loved football—

American and World varieties — tennis, and basketball. In a pinch, he might watch baseball, although it kinda fell right below watching paint dry. Of course, if they ended up with baseball clients, he could hold his own in a conversation about the sport and even spew some stats.

Whatever. So he liked tennis. And Madison Moore.

"Cool it, bro. She's a client," Cole said as he thrust a travel mug of coffee into Derin's hand.

"I know."

Derin ran a hand through his hair and dropped his cowboy hat in place before accepting the coffee. Then he scooped up his keys from the table by the front door of his temporary home, a luxurious double-wide trailer on his newly gifted five-acre piece of land just south of Dylan's. Now that Dylan and Brisa tied the knot, Papi and Mami gifted the four youngest Vargas brothers five acres each for a home. Dalton, the oldest, owned the main ranch house. Even though Dylan's land sat vacant for now, Derin had plans for his own. He had purchased the double-wide the next day, and it had arrived just last week. Man, it was nice not living in the bunkhouse with a bunch of smelly cowboys.

He slid behind the wheel of his dually and backed out as Cole ducked into his fancy lime green McLaren 750S Spider. Derin still couldn't believe Cole willingly gave up his lucrative career as a sports agent to come play second fiddle to him. He also couldn't believe he drove that sweet sports car on the dirt and gravel roads of the ranch. One rock could mar the pristine paint job.

He first met Cole when Cole stayed at the resort — it was how Derin met anyone. Cole was a sports agent, well-connected in tennis, baseball, and football circles. Cole had been looking for the real cowboy experience, and Derin drew the short-straw that day. They became fast friends, keeping in touch via FaceTime and text messages for the past six years. When Cole had downtime, which wasn't often, he came to the ranch. Best part, Cole was a strong Christian — a positive influence — without being overly pious or annoying like Derin's older brothers Dalton and Dylan.

Derin tugged on the collar of the polo shirt again. Cole's business sense far exceeded his own. He would be the better choice to run the sports complex. Not a cowboy with no college education, like Derin.

Didn't matter. He was a Vargas, and Vargases ran every aspect of the guest ranch and resort. Dalton, in his position as Ranch Manager, acted like the CEO of the entire multi-million-dollar enterprise, on track to become billion-dollar. Dylan managed the stables, a job perfect for his quiet older brother. Derin, the middle son, now ran the sports complex. Devon oversaw the children's programming for the resort. And the youngest, Drake, a regular mamacita's boy, ran the coffee shop. Oh, and the dining hall. Their cousin Renata managed the resort and spa.

Derin parked his dually in his assigned parking spot — a paved one — and cut the engine. *We do not deviate from the Lord's plan.* His family's motto replayed in his mind. Maybe this was God's plan. He wasn't sure God could use someone like him. He had one major flaw. One he was getting help with. Between a counselor, a recovery group at a church in town, and Cole as a new roommate, maybe he could straighten himself out and get on with planning his future.

As he flung his truck door open, he noticed the sexy blond — grr, pretty. He was learning his word choices, even the unvoiced ones in his head, mattered. He needed to describe women differently if he really wanted to see them differently and eventually become a man worthy of a wife. So "pretty" or "beautiful" blond. Yeah, he noticed her. She didn't dress like a pro tennis player. Nope. Cute jean shorts topped with a teal ruffle-sleeved shirt made her skin look even more tanned. Dainty sandals. Long golden hair hung down to her waist in bouncy waves. His mouth went dry as he watched the pleasing sway of her hips.

Cole's McLaren parked next to him, the deep purring engine silencing a few seconds later, jolting his eyes from the lovely tennis pro.

"Hey, wait up, Der."

Derin slowed his long legs, giving his shorter friend a chance to catch up.

"You want me to introduce you? I've met Madison before."

"Yeah. What are we going with for my title again?"

"CEO of Vargas Sports."

Derin felt twice as uncomfortable as ten minutes ago. Madison Moore was their first client. He had to make a good first impression, despite his self-doubt. His normal confidence waned. Squaring his shoulders, he decided he should fake it until he made it. He pasted on his most charming grin, straightened his shoulders, and mentally rehearsed his welcome speech as he waited for the introduction.

# 2

---

"MADISON!"

She turned toward the sound of her name and recognized Cole Gregory instantly. Kevin and Syd stood on each side of her as Cole walked up with a cowboy. Well, a cowboy wearing a polo shirt that looked two sizes too small, given how his arms pulled the poor sleeves taut. One sudden move and those seams were toast. Mesmerizing blue eyes stared back at her as she looked up. He had to be a good eight inches taller than her. And those shoulders. How did he walk through a doorway without getting stuck?

"Madison," Kevin started. "You remember Cole Gregory, right?"

"Yeah." Madison's eyes flicked away from the cowboy to the sports agent.

Cole held out his hand for a shake. He stood only an inch or two over her five-foot-eight. His gaze held hers as she curled her fingers around his soft hands.

"Good to see you again, Miss Moore," Cole said, his perfect white teeth glinting in the sun.

"Please, Madison is fine."

"I'm the operations manager here at Vargas Sports. This is Derin Vargas, the CEO of Vargas Sports."

Madison offered the cowboy — er, CEO — a wan smile as she shook his extended, calloused hand. His firm grip startled her. Not what she had expected at all.

"Madison," he said. Then a very charming grin stretched across his handsome, bearded face, sending her pulse skittering. "Please let myself or Cole know if there is anything we can do to make your stay here more pleasant."

She thanked him as Cole introduced Kevin and Sydney. The cowboy oozed confidence as he shook their hands. Madison couldn't help noticing his eyes traveled back to her quickly. Heat warmed her cheeks as she tore her eyes from his.

"I was hoping for a tour before heading over to the casita."

Derin stepped forward. "Right this way."

He held the door for her and her entourage. Once inside, he pointed out all the features of the indoor space. A top-notch gym and locker rooms. Indoor swimming pool for water rehab. Cryo units.

"We have a sports medicine doctor, physical therapist, personal trainer, and chiropractor available for consultation and appointments. Over at the spa, both of our massage therapists are certified for trigger point work," Derin explained. "Of course, you're welcome to a relaxing massage, if you prefer."

"They have mani pedis too," Syd said.

Nice. Madison wouldn't have to leave the resort for a little pampering. Or really, for anything from the sounds of it.

"We also offer custom meals," Cole said. "So let us know your preferences and we'll let the chef know."

"Syd, can you work with them on that?"

"Of course."

They exited the building toward the fenced-in outdoor space. Beautiful desert landscaped berms separated the three immaculate tennis courts from an outdoor basketball court. Bright green grass fields stretched beyond them. One was a full-sized football field. The space included two soccer fields which could also be used for lacrosse.

At the end of the tour, Madison chanced a last glance over her shoulder at the bulky cowboy CEO. Vargas. Clearly a family operation. Yet, based on the tour, they had built a world-class facility with all the most sought after amenities.

Kevin drove them over to the six-bedroom casita, gushing about everything. They had impressed him—a hard feat.

As Madison stepped out of the SUV, she noticed the southwestern feel of the casita. A dark wood door popped against the deep gold exterior. She pressed her key card to the reader. Pushing the door open, her gaze skimmed the great room, which boasted high ceilings with faux wood beams across its creamy paint color. The distressed paint on the walls welcomed her deeper into the room and complemented the beautiful old-world square Spanish tiles on the floor. Gold drapes hung over large windows and a translucent sheer. Light spilled in, brightening the space. The full kitchen included modern quartz countertops and black stainless steel appliances. She would enjoy living there for the next few months.

Madison found her luggage in the largest of the six bedrooms. No surprise there. Her manager and assistant always made sure she could enjoy the privacy of a larger room with an en suite bathroom. As she unpacked her clothes, it bothered her. Was she spoiled? Normal people didn't live like she did.

She snorted. Madison Moore had never lived a normal life. Growing up, she lived on a ranch in Colorado. As the youngest of three kids, she enjoyed the freedom her older brothers hadn't. From a young age, maybe as early as eight, she showed promise as a strong tennis player. Soon afterward, her entire life revolved around the sport. Her first Olympic competition came at the young age of eleven, where she won the gold. Then she competed and won many Junior Nationals events before moving into pro tennis.

Her formative years centered on eating healthy and maintaining the ideal weight. Muscle strengthening. And endless hours of practice. Madison sometimes thought she could literally play tennis in her sleep. Dad and Mom attended as many competitions as they could. They eventually hired a manager for her, since the demands of ranch life limited their ability to arrange things for Madison.

As she hung the last of her blouses on a hanger in the walk-in closet, she bit her lower lip. Over the last few years, her parents hadn't been able to attend most of her matches. But they had hired some cousins to help at the ranch during the US Open so they could fly to New York. They were there for the whole thing.

Madison sighed. After the injury, Mom had shuttled her several hours to the nearest city for her surgery and stayed until the doctor had cleared her to go home. There was nothing her parents wouldn't sacrifice for her. She just hoped she could figure out the next phase of her life so she wouldn't be a burden to them if she couldn't play tennis any longer.

Restless, she left the casita and walked toward the dining hall, enjoying the beautiful sunny day. When she entered the building, her breath caught because of the majestic view. An entire wall of the building opened to patio seating. A tall mountain stood in the distance, beckoning her towards one of the patio tables under the shade of an umbrella.

Madison eased onto the cushioned chair. The bright blue sky loomed overhead. She sighed and snatched the laminated menu from a holder on the table. A tattooed man a few years younger than her stopped by her table.

"Miss Moore, can I get you something?"

Of course, he knew who she was. They must have briefed the staff about her arrival. She resisted rolling her eyes.

"A small iced mocha would be nice. Thanks."

He promised to return shortly with her drink.

Madison flipped over the menu and read the motto printed next to the ranch's brand. *I do not dV8 from the Lord's plan.*

Huh.

She looked around the dining hall and found the same phrase over the door near a verse. *With regard to the works of man, by the word of your lips I have avoided the ways of the violent. My steps have held fast to your paths; my feet have not slipped.*

A blanket of peace settled over her heart. God hadn't left her. He set a path before her and she needed to hold fast to it. If she doubted His concern, His word reminded her He cared. In time, His plan for Madison would become clear. She knew it.

Whether pro tennis remained her career or it became part of her past, God would direct her steps and keep her from slipping.

When the young man set the iced coffee in front of her, she sipped it, soaking up the scenic beauty around her. She allowed her heart to rest secure in God's love.

DERIN'S SECOND OFFICIAL hour of his second official day as the CEO of Vargas Sports, and already he couldn't stand sitting behind the large cherry desk, staring at a computer screen. No wind in his face or sun warming his arms. In another month, his tan would fade and he would look as pale as Devon.

He pushed back from the desk, donned his cowboy hat, and marched out of the building. He headed toward the shed and grabbed the blower. Then he walked to the far tennis court and blew any debris and dirt from the surface. Sure, they had landscapers on staff to do that. But Derin needed to breathe the fresh air of the only office he had known for more than a decade — the vast sky as his ceiling and the sun as his source of light.

A sound nearby caught his attention. He turned to see Madison Moore enter the tennis court with her posse — er, entourage. Whatever. He shut off the blower and scuffed to the edge of the court out of the way.

Madison wore a light yellow tennis skirt showing off her perfectly sculpted long legs. Her white-collar sleeveless top hugged her form. Derin swallowed, unable to rip his gaze away. She bounced the bright tennis ball against the ground, then against her racket. As her partner settled into position on the other side of the court, Madison tossed the ball in the air. Arm stretching high, her racket thwacked it across the court, catching her friend off guard.

A smiled twitched at the corner of Derin's mouth as he watched her wrack up points quickly.

"Don't go easy on me, Coach."

The other woman shook her head. "I'm not trying to. Where's Bella when we need her?"

Madison laughed and Derin thought it a sweet sound, one he could listen to for hours.

In no time at all, Madison won the match against her coach. Another shorter woman in a cute lilac tennis dress joined them. Bella?

"Sorry, I'm late." She unzipped a case and retrieved her racket, twirling it as she spoke. "You didn't mention the place was in the middle of nowhere."

Derin frowned, trying not to take offense at the slight. He inched away from the court and back to the shed, dropping off the blower. He stood there for a second, staring at the door to the building. Unease slithered down his back. Nope. Not yet.

He turned on his heel and strode back to the tennis court. Bella proved to be a better matched opponent for

Madison. Good.

As he watched the two volley the ball from one end of the court to the other, he appreciated Madison's technique. Her overhead smash looked effortless. He knew the level of athleticism needed to pull that off. Her front volley and double-handed backhand strokes were flawless, too. Truly a pro, despite her injury.

When Bella returned Madison's next serve, the ball went low and to Madison's right. He watched something he had never seen from Madison before. She pulled up short, not taking the single backhand stroke he had witnessed dozens of times.

"You had that!" he growled, utterly frustrated by her hesitation. "I've seen you hit more difficult shots in warm-ups. What was that?"

"Who do you think you are?" she hissed, striding toward him. Irritation flashed in her eyes beneath her furrowed brow.

Derin could tell the second she recognized him. Annoyance flipped to fury in two seconds flat.

"What do you know about tennis, cowboy?"

"Plenty. Used to play myself."

Madison scoffed. "Doubt that."

"What? You don't think I know what I'm talking about?"

"I'm a *pro* tennis player!"

Derin stalked toward Bella, determined to prove his point. "Can I borrow your racket?"

"Um. 'Kay." The tiny woman extended it toward him. Then she tossed him a tennis ball, backing away meekly.

"Get ready, Madi. I'll show you how it's done."

Derin tossed the ball in the air and whacked it hard. It bounced on his side of the court before zooming across the net, just out of her reach.

"You got it, Madi!"

"Ah!" She lunged for it and volleyed it back toward him with a vehement, "Ha!"

It sailed toward him, and he backhanded it to her. They smacked the ball back and forth until he saw his opportunity to wing it low with his own overhead smash.

"Go for it, Madi!"

The ball zinged just out of reach to her right. Derin internally rooted for her, knowing she could hit it. Madison dove for the ball with the grit he knew she possessed. Her racket connected with the orb, sending it speeding toward his face. He ducked before striding toward the net, cocky grin firmly in place.

When Derin reached the net, he extended his hand for a shake. Madison vaulted over the net and stood toe to toe with him, her head dropping back to meet his gaze.

Through gritted teeth, she growled, "It's Madison, cowboy."

Derin chuckled for a solid minute. The longer he laughed, her expression morphed from anger to frustration before she stalked away from him.

"Clear the court, cowboy!"

He jogged off, boots clopping against the hard court surface. Glancing over his shoulder just in time, he saw the hint of a smile flit at the corner of her mouth. Yeah, she needed someone like him to challenge her. None of her posse seemed to spur her on to greatness.

Derin mulled over the scene as he walked back to the sports complex. It felt good to help the athlete prove her mettle. He returned to his desk and the awful overhead florescent lights to stare at his computer, still grinning over the encounter.

Later that afternoon, both Cole and Dalton entered his office.

"D4! This is a surprise."

Dalton narrowed his eyes at Derin's nickname for his

oldest brother, Dalton the fourth. A scowl settled on Dalton's face, causing the hair to raise on the back of Derin's neck.

"I heard what you did this morning."

Derin crossed his arms over his chest. "Yeah? Did she thank me?"

Dalton snorted. "No. Her manager threatened to cancel their reservation and book a room at a competitor in Fountain Hills."

Derin's gut squeezed tight as he glanced at Cole. His friend's lips formed a thin line, and he shook his head. Crud. Maybe he *had* overstepped this morning.

"Miss Moore is furious. So is her manager," Cole said. "It took me an hour to calm them down and keep them from leaving."

"Derin, your number one priority is running this place *and* client relations. What you did…" Dalton shook his head. "You need to focus on building up this part of the business. Your behavior was unacceptable."

Derin uncrossed his arms and let them hang limply at his sides. He had really screwed up big time, bigger than when he had nearly lost half the herd when he was seventeen.

Cole cleared his throat. "Miss Moore will stay if you apologize to her. Today. In person."

"So you need to swallow some humble pie and do it, Der." Dalton expelled a loud breath. "Look, I know you can do this job—far better than any of us. I know you'll do the right thing."

Derin nodded and stood, ignoring his churning stomach. "You got it, D4. I'll fix it."

As he moved past his brother, a firm hand clamped down on his shoulder. "I'll pray for you."

Derin frowned and stormed from the building. It would take more than his brother's prayers to fix this. He knew what he had to do. He could be charming when he wanted to. Even if it required him to swallow his pride.

# 3

---

"DERIN VARGAS IS here," Syd said as she cracked open the door to Madison's room.

"I'll meet him on the porch."

Madison waited for Syd to close the door, fully intending to make the bossy cowboy with too much swagger wait on her. She was in no hurry to see or speak to him again. She couldn't believe she let Cole talk her into this. Madison removed the ice pack from her shoulder before she stretched it. It hurt less than she had expected after those difficult shots from Derin.

The handsome man, with his sparkling blue eyes and rugged charm, was insufferable.

Madi. She scoffed at his nickname for her as she pushed off the easy chair.

Madison had to credit him for doing what no one else had. He made her mad enough and ignited her competitive spirit so much that she forgot to worry about her shoulder. All she had cared about during that match was proving him wrong. In doing so, she achieved a new milestone in her recovery. One that Layla, Kevin, and Bella failed to bring out in her.

Derin Vargas gave her the one victory that calmed her anxious thoughts and confronted her fears quietly.

Huh.

Madi.

A smile twitched at the corner of her mouth. No one had ever used that nickname for her, either. Yet, for some stupid reason, she liked it when the cowboy CEO said it.

Madison trudged to the fridge and tossed the ice pack in the freezer. Then she popped the lid off two fruity seltzers and carried them by the bottles' necks in one hand as she walked toward the front of the casita.

She eased the door open, glimpsing the cowboy's back as he leaned against the railing of the front porch. The sun setting behind him highlighted his brawny physique. He looked fresh off the cover of some western billboard for a rodeo.

"I'm sorry, Madi." He cleared his throat. "Miss Moore."

She sidled up next to him, offering one bottle. His thick, calloused fingers brushed against hers as he accepted the peace offering, igniting waves of fire through her. The cool evening air brushed against her skin, but it didn't send a chill down her spine after the contact with Derin. His cologne smelled amazing and oh so masculine. She moved a few paces away and scooted onto the top of the log railing, feet dangling between the vertical rungs.

"Call me Madison." She tossed her head back as she gulped the watermelon seltzer.

"Madison. I… I'm still getting used to this new job."

That confession surprised her. She angled her head to look at him. "Oh?"

"I used to be the foreman of a bunch of crude, ornery cowboys. It takes a certain direct, firm approach to wrangle them."

Madison watched as he chugged a third of the beverage. Humble looked good on him.

"I realize I significantly overstepped with you today."

She snorted, not wanting to let him off too easy. "You think?"

He turned to face her now, muscular shoulder still leaning against the log pillar of the porch. "Yeah, I think."

He pushed off from the pillar.

"I had no business meddling with your practice. It's just that…"

Derin's lips clamped together, and Madison took a little pity on him.

"It's just what?"

"I've seen you play. Saw you at the US Open and I know what you're capable of."

Heat spread across her face. Thankfully, dusk would keep him from seeing any color on her cheeks. She hoped.

"I know what it's like to be paralyzed with fear."

Madison felt her ire rising again. "I doubt that."

Derin reached out and clasped her hand, sending thrilling shivers up her spine. "I do. Trust me."

When he released her hand, Madison stared at him for a few seconds. The porch light flicked on and she noticed the sincerity in his eyes. Gorgeous, moody blue eyes. She could drown in them.

Derin cleared his throat. "I know I'm botching this apology. I wasn't trying to overstep. You're capable of great things, and I thought you needed a nudge — one that your confidants wouldn't provide. Even so, it was not my place to be the one to do it. I hope you'll stay and make use of our facilities. I'll steer clear of you."

He downed the rest of the drink and turned toward the parking spaces.

"Wait!" Madison inwardly cringed as the word ripped from her mouth against her will. She did not know what possessed her to forgive him.

"Thank you, Derin."

He touched his fingertips to the brim of his cowboy hat and walked further away, his large body shadowed by the darkness of night.

"And," she said, jogging up to him, "thanks for pushing me. You're right. I was so afraid of re-injuring my shoulder that I held back."

Derin spun to face her with wide eyes. She clasped her hands in front of her and shifted from foot to foot.

"You were right. Though I don't recommend treating your other clients like this."

He chuckled, a deep toe-curling sound that was growing on her.

"Good night, Madi," he tossed over his shoulder as he strode away.

Madison stood there rooted in place as she watched him climb into his dually. The enormous truck fit the cowboy, just like the hat, jeans, boots, and the huge belt buckle. She didn't know Derin Vargas well, but he was all cowboy.

What had he said? That he was new to the whole CEO thing. Yeah, easy to believe that. As he drove away, she wondered what prompted him to take on the new job.

And just why did she care?

She shook off the thoughts and went inside the casita, trying to forget about the intriguing cowboy.

DERIN EASED BEHIND the wheel of his dually. Turning the key, the engine roared awake. He drove away from the casitas before letting out a loud breath. Yeah. He almost botched the apology, too. He cracked the window, allowing the chilly evening air to flow through his truck.

Something definitely passed between him and Madi. It bothered him. She affected him like no one ever had. He didn't know what caused him to provoke her. His gut told him she needed someone to motivate her beyond the fear on the tennis court.

At least he managed enough of an apology that she wouldn't leave and they wouldn't lose the business. Derin hated the thought that he almost lost their very first client.

That fear he mentioned? Yeah. It was his present battle. Trying to defeat the voices that told him he could never change. He would never be good enough for his job.

Derin pressed the accelerator, kicking up a cloud of dust behind him. He needed to get home before he changed his mind and found escape in the arms of a random woman. Those old patterns of dealing with his failures and fears would only set him back. Eight months of barely succeeding at recovery. He couldn't throw it all away on one mistake.

When he parked his truck by his temporary home, he cut the engine and sat there. The war waged inside of him. It would be so easy to turn around and head back to the resort. Hang out at the dining hall. Schmooze some pretty single lady. Feel the heat. Numb his failures in fleeting pleasure.

Yeah, and then not be able to look at himself in the mirror tomorrow.

From what Derin had learned in his recovery group, any vice of the flesh shared similar challenges. The drive to escape, whether it was through food, alcohol, drugs, or, in his case, sex, required continual recommitment to sobriety. He had a choice. He could choose escape—to give in to the temptation. Or he could choose to abstain. Even in the most perfect of moments when he surrendered his heart to God, he still struggled with the lure. Still had to make a choice. And if he decided not to make a choice, he still made one— one that usually involved falling back on more than a decade of bad patterns.

A knock rapped on the window, startling him from his brooding. Derin glanced to see Cole standing there. He eased the door open and grabbed his hat from the dash before closing it. One small choice made. In the right direction.

"You okay?" Cole asked.

"No." His gut ached with anxiety.

"Come inside. I brought back extra food from the dining hall. We can turn on the sports channel and argue with the analysts."

Derin chortled, following his friend into the house. Cole always had known how to cheer him up.

The sound of one of his favorite shows floated through the house. It picked apart the latest football playoff game from last Saturday, citing the quarterback as the problem on the losing team. The show provided the distraction Derin needed.

"Were they even watching the game? It's not the quarterback's fault when the O-line didn't protect him."

Cole retrieved a plate of food and popped it into the microwave. "There's my best friend."

Derin shrugged. "Maybe my new coping mechanism could be yelling at these morons."

"Eh. Better not trade one problem for another. Besides, you've always been opinionated."

"Yeah, there is that."

Cole handed him silverware and the warm plate. The scent of meatloaf and mac n cheese filled the surrounding air, making his mouth water. Derin settled onto his plush leather couch and listened to the show while he ate. Cole sat on the other end, propping his bare feet on the coffee table.

"You think they'll release the receiver that is on injured reserve?" Cole asked.

Derin swallowed a bite of moist meatloaf before answering. "They should. He hasn't been good for a few years now."

"He used to be a client."

Derin frowned, surprised by the sadness in his friend's tone. Guess he wasn't the only one still adjusting to his new job.

"Do you miss it?"

Cole sipped his soda before shrugging. "Yes, and no. I'm tired of the road life. Following players all over the country. Working my butt off for their weird proclivities."

"Such big words for a jock."

"Ha, ha. Anyway, I'm glad to be here. You and me, we'll figure out what running the sports complex looks like. I had another former client recommend us to a friend. I asked Renata to let me know if they book a visit."

Derin appreciated everything Cole was doing. Using his contacts to help build the business. Challenging Derin when he overstepped.

"How did she take it?"

"Madi? Like a champ."

Cole raised an eyebrow. Derin straightened and flashed a grin.

"Come on. I'm charming."

Cole tossed a throw pillow at his head, but Derin batted it to the floor.

"Seriously, she understood and is gonna stay. She even thanked me for pushing her past her fear."

"You have great instincts," Cole admitted. "Now we just have to channel it so it doesn't get us fired."

"I half expected you to tell me to learn to shut my mouth."

Cole laughed. "First, I know that's a lost cause. You are who you are. Second, athletes sometimes need an objective third-party to motivate them. To point out what their friends and coaches won't. We cater to rehabbing athletes. Sometimes, to help them, we might have to risk speaking the truth."

"I know, I know," Derin said, holding up his hands. "But speak it in love, as Mami would say."

"Exactly."

Derin stood and strode into the kitchen, scraping the last bits of his meal into the trash. Then he loaded the dishes into the dishwasher.

"Cole?"

"Huh?"

"Thanks for watching my back today."

"Any time, bro."

# 4

THE NEXT MORNING, Derin entered the complex in gym shorts and a special athletic shirt Cole raved about. Staring at the equipment in the high-end gym, he frowned. The entire idea of working out felt dumb. He had never done it outside of high school. He worked on a ranch. That had always built his muscles and made him strong without trying.

But Cole had an excellent point. Derin's new job involved a lot less physical activity than Derin was used to. So, he convinced him to join the ranks of people who worked out.

Derin blew out a breath, feeling intimidated and overwhelmed by the equipment. Sure, he had approved all the purchases, but the physical therapist and personal trainer on staff picked it out. He only had a vague idea of how to use some of it.

"Just staring at it does nothing, cowboy."

A female voice laughed behind him, startling him. He whirled around to see Madi's sardonic smile. Derin allowed himself a few seconds to take in her athletic tank-top and gym shorts. Those pretty brown eyes. Long blond hair pulled back into a ponytail. One bright pink earbud in her left ear, the other probably in her closed hand.

He leaned against the rail of a treadmill. "What's your preference?"

"Today is the bike for cardio before arms for weights. Tomorrow will be the treadmill and legs."

At the mention of her legs, his eyes darted to them before he quickly snapped his eyes back to hers. "Looks like they'll survive another day."

"You don't impress me as a workout kind of guy," she quipped as she settled onto the recumbent bike in front of the row of treadmills.

Derin stepped onto a treadmill where he could still see her and not be right behind her. That just seemed cringe. "First time."

She looked over her shoulder at him, already pedaling hard. "You're not serious!"

"Ranch work is physically demanding. Never needed to spend more time expending energy."

"Ah, but the new job."

"Yeah."

"Enjoy your workout," she said before she popped in the other earbud.

Derin blinked at all the options on the treadmill. Incline. Speed. Varied workout. Fast workout. Sheesh. He would have to ask Cole about it later. Or maybe let the personal trainer practice on him when he didn't have clients to work with. He punched the quick start, and the belt jerked, nearly sending his face careening into the control panel until he started walking. He mashed the speed button higher until he settled into an easy jog.

After three minutes, the sound of his own thoughts annoyed him, and he understood why Madi wore earbuds. Music, an audiobook, or anything would be better than just thinking.

His eyes slid to Madi. After twenty minutes, she moved on to the circuit weights and used several machines for her upper body and arms. She seemed to be a pro at this gym stuff, too.

Whatever had passed between them last night seemed more muted today. At least she hadn't run from the gym when she noticed him there. Maybe she had forgiven him for yesterday.

"Hey, Derin!"

Derin nodded to Hudson, the personal trainer who looked like he lived in the gym most days. The guy, though kinda on the short side, didn't have an ounce of fat on his body.

"You want to try some weights?"

Derin punched the stop button on the treadmill, breathing hard as sweat dripped down his back. He followed Hudson to the free weights.

"Cole said you might want advice about weight training."

Wouldn't hurt to try it. He listened as Hudson explained how to set up the weights and the importance of always having a spotter for free weights, like the bench press.

"The last thing you need is for this bar to drop on your chest. Trust me on that."

"How much weight did you put on here?" he asked as he laid on the bench.

"I figured we'd see how two-hundred feels. Ready?"

Derin grunted. He placed his hands on the cold metal bar like Hudson showed him, wondering where Madi ran off to. Then he lifted it to remove the bar from the holder. He eased it down, not feeling a thing.

"Yeah, I thought it might be too light." Hudson secured the bar and added more weight. "Two-forty."

Derin felt the burn in his chest and arms as he eased his arms up and down against the resistance of the weights.

"Hey, Madison! You want me to tape up your shoulder?" The sound of the physical therapist's voice seemed close by.

"Sure. Thanks, Ryan."

"You'll need to take off your shirt."

Derin nearly dropped the bar at the image conjured in his mind. Heat spread over his face as Hudson grabbed the bar and set it on the holder.

"Easy there. That's probably enough reps for today."

Derin sat up slowly, hoping his face didn't look as red as it felt. His eyes scanned the room and saw the top of Ryan's head on the other side of a divider. Guess they had a semi-private area for taping up shoulders.

He took the offered towel from Hudson, wiping it across his too fiery face.

"Next week, we can focus on other muscle groups and we'll see what works best for you."

"Thanks, bro."

Derin stood, hurrying from the gym to the locker room and a cold shower. Maybe that would redirect his crazy thoughts.

After he showered and changed into jeans, boots, a solid button-down shirt, and his hat, he felt human again. He joined Cole in the conference room, where they interviewed a guest services specialist—a fancy name for the person who would work at the front desk of the complex and help with a variety of tasks. As soon as that interview concluded, they interviewed for a few other open positions.

Sometimes Derin wondered if their plan was a little too aggressive. It made him uncomfortable to hire so much staff, with only Madi staying there.

"Renata said we've had three more extended stay bookings. Two are pro football players and they booked one of the six-bedroom casitas to share. They plan to stay for three months. Maybe longer."

"That's great news. When do they check in?" Derin asked.

Cole grinned. "Next week."

"Oh. Guess it's a good thing we're hiring all these people."

"Told you we would need them. There's also a baseball player and a woman's basketball player coming in two or three weeks."

"How did they hear about us?"

"Madison posted something on her social media account. Guess she's acquaintances with the basketball player. The rest are friends of my former clients or friends of friends."

"Thanks, bro. This is a great start."

"Just glad to be here, trying something new."

They went their separate ways for the rest of the afternoon. At the end of his day, Derin texted Cole to let him know he had a recovery group meeting that evening. Then he drove into Wickenburg, parking outside of the small church—a different one from his family's church.

One guy from his group pulled up next to him and they walked in for the meeting together. Derin took a seat in the circle. After the leader prayed for the group, he listened to Jeff's latest struggles.

When it was his turn, he took a minute to gather his thoughts.

"How do you handle dating?" Derin asked. "And not..."

His gut knotted. He still had a hard time talking about any of this. But he needed some strategy to navigate a relationship. Huh. He was actually thinking about a relationship and not a hookup. Guess that was progress.

A thirty-something guy with a wife and two kids spoke up. "When I started dating my wife—before she was my wife—I told her about my problems. She came up with this great idea. One hundred and one questions." Derin stared at him blankly and he laughed. "I know it sounds weird. You can find a ton of apps like that online. Just download one on your phone and use them as a guide. It kept us from focusing too much on attraction. And it helped us get to know each other quickly."

"One hundred and one questions?"

"Yeah, I'll send you a link to one. We still buy these now and then. Gives us a place to start a conversation."

Derin frowned as the guy tapped on his phone several times.

"Here's one: What's one place you've always wanted to visit and haven't yet?"

Derin cocked his head to one side, the suggestion finally making sense.

Jeff piped up. "Oh, I like it. Takes the pressure off what to say."

"Yeah. And you focus on getting to know the other person."

Derin ran a hand over his beard. One hundred and one questions. Hmm. He wondered what Madi would think about that.

MADISON HELD BACK a giggle as she entered the gym. For the third day in a row, she and Derin seemed to be on the same workout schedule. Today he sat on the recumbent bike, earbuds in, huffing hard. He hadn't seen her yet, so she walked in front of him and nodded to him. He raised a hand in a little wave. She left an empty bike between them when she sat down. She popped in her earbuds and played loud music.

Forty minutes later, she looked around for Derin, but she didn't see him anymore. He must have finished while she focused on the bike. He hadn't said goodbye and that disappointed her.

Madison held back a snort. Why did it matter? It's not like they were friends or anything. He had said he would steer clear of her the other day. For some strange reason, she didn't really want him to. She thought he understood that the first day she saw him in the gym.

When she finished her weight training, Madison retrieved her racket from the locker room before walking over to the tennis court. She texted Bella and Layla to let them know she was on her way. When she arrived, Layla had the tennis ball machine loaded up. She groaned. She hated the machine.

"Bella is on her way, but stuck in traffic," Layla explained, patting the top of the machine. "So, this here will be her substitute until she arrives."

Madison dropped her duffle bag on the edge of the court. Then she faced off against it. It lobbed ball after ball toward her, varying by distance and angle. She hit every ball back, sometimes lunging low to hit one.

Between the machine and her workout, she was exhausted. By the time Bella arrived, Madison wished she could call it a day. Layla wouldn't have it.

"You've got six weeks before the tournament. We're going to host a mock tournament here in two."

"Fine."

Madison served first, wailing the ball hard across the court. Bella volleyed it back. After three matches, Madison was in a foul mood. Bella trounced her all three times. Talk about discouraging.

"Hey," Layla said, matching her pace on the path to the parking lot. "You can't win them all. So we practice. It helps us see where to focus our efforts."

"I'm never going to be ready for the tournament."

"Not with that attitude. Remember," Layla tapped a finger on her temple. "Most of the battle is up here. Get your mind right. Enjoy the weekend off and we'll pick it up on Monday."

Madison's shoulders slumped as she thanked her coach

and her friend. Then she trudged back to the casita. The sun's rays warmed her back as the cloudless blue sky hung overhead.

What would she do if she couldn't play tennis? Tennis had been her life for so long. Without tennis, who was Madison Moore?

She nudged the casita door open and scuffed to her room, closing the door behind her. After letting the water warm up, she entered the steamy shower. By the time Madison finished her hot shower, she felt no better about her situation. Since it was almost time for dinner, she put on some makeup, curled her hair, and walked down to the dining hall.

She had given Sydney the day off, especially since there really wasn't much for her personal assistant to do. Kevin had flown home to spend a few weeks with his family. He planned to come back the week of the tournament.

She pushed open the dining hall door and the savory smell of home cooked food greeted her. The garlic and herb scent reminded her of her mother's oven-baked roast beef and potatoes. A pang of homesickness washed over her. When was the last time she even visited the ranch? Or saw her brothers?

"Evening, Madi."

A smile twitched at the corner of her mouth. She turned to greet Derin, wishing she could think of some snarky nickname for him.

"Cowboy."

Oh, and did he ever look the part. Checkered shirt. Big silver belt buckle sparkling in the light. Fitted jeans. Hat. Boots. Was it hot in here?

"Got any exciting plans for the weekend?"

Madison exhaled loudly as she took a plate at the front of the buffet line. She normally ate lots of protein and veggies, avoiding carbs. But tonight she felt like splurging a little. Roast beef, mashed potatoes, gravy. And a small side salad to assuage the guilt.

"Nope. Two whole days of nothing."

"Not even practice?"

"Layla gave me the weekend off after an abysmal practice today."

A grin spread across his face as he held out a chair for her at a small table. For two.

"Go line dancing with me."

"Bossy much?" Madison arched an eyebrow to hide how much the idea excited her.

Derin hitched his shoulder. "You need to get out. Have some fun. Take your mind off tennis for an evening."

"I don't know." She caught her lower lip between her teeth.

Derin held out his hand and asked, "Mind if I pray?"

The question surprised her. He hadn't impressed her as a devout man. Madison nodded as she slipped her hand in his. He bowed his head, offering thanks for their food and the company. When Derin finished, she considered his invitation.

"Fine. I'll go with you."

Somehow, he grinned around the bite of food in his mouth. He pulled his phone from his shirt pocket, swiping and tapping a few times. Then he looked up, expression serious, and asked the most bizarre question.

"If you were stranded on a deserted island and could choose any three things to have with you, what would you pick and why?"

"What?" Her eyes rounded.

"You heard the question, Madi."

She chewed slowly, mulling it over.

"That's hard."

"Right?" He chuckled.

"What would you pick?"

"No dodging it. I'll answer after you do."

"Ugh. Let's assume I have food and water."

Derin narrowed his eyes and conceded.

"My Bible."

He rolled his eyes.

"What? It's a legit answer."

"So says every church goer. Next?"

"You wouldn't?"

He wagged a finger at her as he stabbed a chunk of roast before popping it in his mouth.

"Chocolate."

Derin tossed his head back and chuckled loudly. So much so that a few heads turned their direction. "Women."

"And a Costco-sized bag of ground coffee."

"How are you making the coffee?"

"I don't know. I'm sure I could figure it out."

Madison pushed her empty plate away. "Your turn."

"First choice? You."

Heat flamed her cheeks. What was he saying?

"Second choice would be Djano."

Madison quirked an eyebrow.

"My horse. And that's only because you put the stipulation that food and water aren't an issue. So, he won't starve."

She snorted. "Me and your horse."

"Yup. And my hat. That's it."

"Me, your horse, and your hat." She shook her head. "Why me?"

Derin's eyes glinted with mirth. "You're insanely beautiful. Smart. Very entertaining."

Her cheeks warmed at the compliment.

"We would fight like cats and dogs."

He shook his head. "I'm not buying that."

"I can't stand you."

"Not buying that either." Derin pushed back from the table, grabbing her hand. "Come on. We've gotta go if we're going to make it to line dancing on time."

"Is that a rigidly scheduled activity?"

Derin chuckled. "See, why wouldn't I pick you and your snarky sense of humor to keep me company on a deserted island?"

Madison let him hurry her to his truck, enjoying the feel of his hand clasped around hers. This cowboy confused her. Sent her pulse thrumming, leaving her breathless. Pushed her buttons. Yet, somehow, he had made her happiness this evening his priority.

Derin held the truck door open for her. She climbed in and buckled up while he crossed to the driver's side. When he settled behind the wheel, he unlocked his phone and swiped the screen on an app.

"Here's another one. Have you ever won an award for a sport?"

Madison snatched up the phone. "Huh. That's really the question. What is this?"

"One hundred and one questions to ask on a date."

"Is this a date?"

"Welcome to the party, Madi."

Heat warmed her face. Derin was one of a kind. She shook her head and handed him his phone. He set it on the holder before backing out.

"Answer the question, Madi. Have you ever won an award for a sport?"

She snorted. "You know I have."

"So tell me about them. We've got about a thirty-minute drive to town. You think you can list them all off by then?"

"You asked for it, cowboy."

# 5

DERIN COULD NOT stop grinning as he drove to his favorite country bar and restaurant in Wickenburg. The place had live music and line dancing on Friday nights. It had been ages since he had gone out on a Friday. And longer since he went on a real date.

So far, the questions app was working perfectly. He listened as Madi started with her first award at ten. Olympic medals. Junior tournaments. Pro awards. No surprises there, as he knew she was accomplished in tennis. The one award that baffled him had nothing to do with tennis.

"First place at a craft fair?" he asked. "For what?"

"My mother taught me how to knit."

Derin snorted. "Knitting?"

"What? It's a useful skill. Maybe not in Arizona. But in Colorado, knitting scarfs, hats, and sweaters is a necessity."

"What did you knit?"

When he glanced over, he noticed her ducked head. She picked at something on her jeans.

"A toaster cover."

"A first place toaster cover?" He shook his head.

"Yup. I was only eight."

"Oh, I'm sure that makes all the difference."

"So, how about you? Have you won any awards for a sport or anything?"

"Junior rodeo. I've got a few buckles from bronc riding."

"But you didn't go pro?"

"Naw. I'm a Vargas. We own a ranch. So, I knew I'd be working with my family."

"Do you wish you would have tried?"

Derin thought about it for a second. "Nope. I love what I do." That tightness in his chest reminded him he didn't love his new job. Not yet. Maybe in time, when he felt more comfortable with it. "What I used to do."

"You miss it."

"Yeah."

"So, why the change?"

Derin pulled into the parking lot and shut off the truck, grateful for the opportunity to avoid the subject.

"We're here."

The muffled sound of country music spilled into the parking lot as he hopped out of his truck. He circled the front to get her door. After he closed the door behind her, he held her hand. The music grew louder as he led her into the bar.

"Ready to dance?"

Madi giggled shyly. "It's been years."

"But you have line danced before?"

"I grew up on a ranch in Colorado."

Derin's head dropped to the side. "I don't think I knew that."

"I'm a country girl at heart."

Warmth spread through him as his pulse quickened. "You ride?"

"Yeah."

Smart. Gorgeous. Country gal. Horse woman. And a pro athlete. Could she be any more perfect?

Derin shook off the thoughts and escorted her to the dance floor as a song began. He kept Madi to his right. He grinned as *Tucson Too Late* blared from the speakers.

"I don't think I know this one." She laughed nervously, tucking her hair behind her ear.

"You've got this. Step, step, step-shuffle step."

Madi missed the shuffle part and bumped his side, giggling as her perfume sent his pulse racing. "Sorry."

He hooked his thumbs in his belt loops as he turned along with the crowd. Madi almost crashed into him again. He winked at her.

"Other way."

She quickly twirled and stepped. By their third time through the pattern, Madi grinned just before the twirl. Derin's heart felt weightless within his chest, and he wished for a few more seconds to memorize her look of pure joy.

When the song ended, she touched his forearm and leaned forward, giddy. She laughed, and she vibrated with enthusiasm. He beamed, pleased with her reaction.

"That was so fun!"

The next dance started. Her eyes lit up and her back straightened.

"I know this one."

Derin enjoyed the whiff of her sweet perfume as Madi took her place beside him. They moved in perfect harmony with the rest of the dancers. Derin let loose, with a little more swing in his hips to match Madi's style. He couldn't remember the last time he enjoyed line dancing like he hadn't a care in the world.

After the third song, the DJ played a slower one. Derin faced Madi, his heart racing. A soft smile stretched across her lips, so he pulled her close, swaying to the gentle beat of the music. When she slid her hands up his arms and rested them behind his neck, he swallowed hard. She must like him if she initiated a closer hold than he had. He placed his hands lightly at her waist, heart beating so loud he could hear it over the music.

Her fragrance heightened his senses. When she pressed

closer, he stilled. Fire coursed through him, stirring all kinds of inappropriate ideas—remnants from the life he didn't want any more. Derin released his hold. He lightly held her shoulders and spun her toward the bar.

"I could use a soda. Want anything?"

He noticed her shock. Hopefully, Madi wouldn't read his reaction as rejection. He liked her and the very last thing he wanted to do was treat her like the string of women from his past. There was something about Madi that made him want to treat her like a princess. She deserved a man far better than him.

"Derin, are you okay?"

He hitched a shoulder. "Yeah. Just thirsty."

Her brown eyes studied him for a second. "I'll take a Sprite."

"Wanna find us a table?"

Derin didn't wait for an answer before he left her and strode toward the bar. He ordered their drinks, taking a minute to text his support group for prayer cover.

He turned and scanned the tables for her. Across the distance, her eyes latched on to his. Like a punch to the gut, his breath whooshed from his lungs. Madi was in a different class of gorgeous. It almost hurt to look at her, long golden hair spilling over her shoulder in silky waves.

The war inside of Derin threatened to tear him apart. He would love to take her to his bed. Except it would destroy everything. She was special. He knew it from the night he apologized to her. Her capacity to forgive his brazen mocking on the tennis court humbled him. No other woman compared to Madi. Jumping to the physical with her would ruin anything good that might develop between them. And for some perplexing reason, he longed for that something good more than the fleeting physical pleasure.

Yeah. Whoever thought prayer didn't work had to be nuts. 'Cause thoughts like this? They definitely came from his prayers and those of his group. They certainly didn't come from his remarkably weak flesh.

"Your drinks," the bartender said, sliding the glasses across the glossy bar top.

Derin grabbed them and ambled toward Madi at the high-top, mind spinning through ways to increase his self-control tonight. Slow dances had to be off-limits unless they two-stepped with a saintly distance between them. No goodnight kiss. More of those one hundred and one questions.

*Lord, my heart is willing to live differently, but I am so very, very weak. Please protect Madi from me.*

MADISON TRIED NOT to feel hurt by Derin's abrupt end to their slow dance. Had she misread his interest? Did she move too fast by hooking her hands behind his neck?

She shook her head slightly as a couple vacated a high-top table. She hopped onto the seat and watched Derin walk toward the bar.

Over the years, she had dated a few guys. But the last time she had slow danced must have been in high school. If dancing with her hands behind his neck and his hands on her waist was acceptable for teenagers, surely it was appropriate for adults.

So what did it mean that Derin practically bolted off the dance floor at her touch?

He turned and searched the crowd for her. When he spotted her, their eyes locked. She saw a storm there. Conflict within himself. His gaze flicked to some distant point behind her.

Maybe his abrupt shift had nothing to do with her.

*Lord, give me wisdom in whatever this is. Help me let him*

*lead.*

As Derin walked toward Madison with two glasses in his hand, a friendly smile appeared. She returned it.

"Here you go."

He set the Sprite in front of her, and she thanked him. She sipped it as he eased into the chair across from her. Derin sipped his dark soda, staring at the tabletop.

"How often do you go dancing?" she asked, trying to ease the tension between them.

"Hardly ever. Been too busy."

"You're good at it."

"Thanks."

When his gaze darted to the dance floor, an awkward silence hung over them. Madison hoped the evening wouldn't end so soon. She couldn't remember the last time she had enjoyed herself so much. And with no paparazzi flashing cameras in her face.

"It's kind of nice no one recognizes me."

Derin snorted, his eyes finally connecting with hers. "Few folks around here follow tennis. I'm probably odd that I do."

"And why do you?"

His face reddened. "I played tennis in high school and really enjoyed it. Played football too."

Madison laughed. "Football I can picture. Tennis — well, only because you played against me and clearly knew what you were doing."

He downed the rest of his soda.

"Ready?" he asked, holding his hand out for her.

After she polished off her drink, she placed her hand in his and followed him out for another line dance. They danced side by side for most of the line dances. When the next slow song played, he hesitated. Madison prepared to feign needing a trip to the bathroom. But he held his hand out and suggested two-stepping. Whatever fear she felt earlier melted away. He wanted to dance with her. Close, but not too close. She didn't have to understand it to respect it. For the remaining slow songs, they did the same thing. She graciously followed his lead.

When she yawned, Derin suggested taking her home. It had been a long day for both of them.

On the drive back, Madison swiped through several straightforward questions from the app.

"Favorite ice cream?"

"Oreo," he said. "You?"

"Chocolate with caramel."

"Not surprised, Miss Bible, chocolate, and lifetime supply of coffee gal."

Madison giggled before asking the next question. "Favorite color?"

"Blue."

Even though it was too dark to see his mesmerizing blue eyes, she could agree. At last, she said, "Teal."

"Really? Never would have guessed."

"Hey!"

"Come on, Madi. You wore teal at least three times this week."

It surprised her he had noticed. A flutter danced in her stomach, and she giggled to hide how much his comment affected her. "Okay, so maybe I have too many teal workout shirts."

When they settled into a comfortable silence, he thumped the button to turn on his radio, letting country music play softly in the background. She looked out the window, unable to make out anything beyond the glow of his truck's headlights. Before she knew it, he parked in front of her casita.

Madison held her breath as Derin opened the truck door for her. She had a great time with him. Better than she would have imagined, except for him cutting off that first slow dance quickly. He refused to talk about it, but he two-stepped with her a few times. She wondered what it all meant. Maybe it meant nothing at all.

When Derin walked her to the door of the casita, she turned to face him.

"Thanks for the fun date."

A smile turned up one side of his bearded face. His eyes darkened, and she wished she could see them better. Unfortunately, the porch light was off. He stood a few inches away from her. The air sparked between them and she leaned forward slightly to let him know if he wanted to kiss her, she would be open to it.

Several seconds ticked by as the energy zinged between them. Then he jammed his hands in his pockets, stepping back.

"Night, Madi. I had a great time."

"Me too."

Neither of them moved.

"Well, I should go," he said.

Still, neither so much as flinched.

"Night," she whispered, resigning herself to no kiss. It was probably better not to, anyway. She was here to rehab, after all.

Then Madison turned away, placing her key card on the pad. She heard his boots thud on the porch. The sound of his truck echoed in the still night air before the casita door closed behind her.

Madison leaned against the closed door. What was she doing staring at the broad-shouldered cowboy? Inviting him to kiss her? She was there for her career, not a relationship with the CEO of the sports complex.

Ugh. She had too much on her plate as it was. Why try to complicate it further?

As she snuggled into bed, the feel of his hands on her waist lingered in her mind. She fell asleep to dreams of what a kiss from Derin might have felt like.

# 6

---

DERIN COULD GET used to spending time with Madison Moore. And he definitely would choose her if he was ever stranded on an island, despite her affinity for chocolate. A half-smile tilted his lips.

As he shifted his truck into reverse, he tamped down his fiery attraction. An important milestone just occurred in his recovery. He walked away without even so much as a kiss, despite wanting to kiss her and so much more. Maybe, just maybe, Derin could learn how to have a relationship with a woman. Maybe it could turn into something lasting.

He shook his head as he parked his truck in front of his home. Even thinking about a relationship seemed like rushing things.

The porch light flicked on. He didn't have motion sensors on there, which meant Cole had been waiting for him. Irritation bubbled up. Though he shouldn't be upset. He had asked Cole to hold him accountable. His friend was only doing what he had asked him to do.

Derin jumped out of his truck, shoving the door shut and arming it. He strode toward the house, trying to control his unfounded irritation.

"Evening," he said as he entered.

"How was your date with Madison?" Cole asked, frowning. With arms crossed over his chest, he leaned against the doorjamb of his room.

"Good. We went dancing."

"Yeah, Syd said as much."

Derin's head jerked back. "You checking up on me?"

Cole's face turned red as he uncrossed his arms, letting them hang at his sides. "No. I, uh, took Syd out to dinner."

"What?" Derin could scarcely believe it.

"Yeah. She's really nice. Christian. Pretty."

A grin spread across Derin's face. "Cole Gregory went on a date. With a client."

"Nope. She's not a client. She works for a client. Big difference."

"If you say so."

"You're the one dating a client."

Derin heard the warning in Cole's tone. "Yeah, just dating, bro. We went line dancing. Kept my distance on the slow songs."

"You kiss her?"

Derin scoffed. "You kiss her assistant?"

"Not hardly. It was our first date."

"Well, same here."

Cole held his gaze for a few seconds. Then he nodded sharply. "Glad to hear it. I'm gonna call it a night."

"Night, bro."

Derin strode to the fridge and poured himself a glass of water. Then he entered his bedroom. Sitting on the edge of his bed, he expelled a loud breath. He did it. Dated a woman and had fun without so much as a kiss. He set the water on his nightstand before retrieving his phone. Then he fired off a text, thanking the guys for the prayer cover.

After climbing under the covers, he thanked God for this one monumental victory.

As Derin turned off his light, he decided he would surprise Madi tomorrow with a treat. He just hoped she would like it as much as he thought she would.

THE NEXT MORNING, Madison woke to her phone pinging with multiple messages. She groaned and rolled onto her side, lazily unlocking it, while pushing her hair out of her face.

*Wakey, wakey.*

*Time to get up.*

*We're waiting.*

Madison frowned at the unfamiliar number. *Who are you?*

*Derin.*

She growled as her fingers punched back a response. *Who are we?*

*Me. Cole. Sydney.*

Madison threw back the covers as she pulled up her calendar. Nothing on it. She texted Syd. *Did I miss an appointment?*

Sydney: *No. Your boyfriend wanted to surprise you.*

Madison: *I don't have a boyfriend.*

Derin: *She means me.*

Ugh. It wasn't a group chat, but apparently, Syd had relayed her messages.

Derin: *Wear a cowgirl outfit.*

The nerve!

She sent back an angry, blowing top emoji before tossing her phone on her bed. Then she changed into jeans, a top, and her cowgirl boots before pulling her hair back at the base of her neck. She jammed her cowgirl hat on her head, stuffing her phone and room key in her back pocket as she hurried toward the front door of the casita.

When Madison flung the door open, Derin grinned that cocky smile of his while he eased down from his black horse.

"Sleeping beauty arrives at last!"

"You know, if you want someone to be ready for an outing, you can ask ahead of time. It's called scheduling."

Derin's deep chuckle warmed her to her toes. She fought against her own smile, wanting to stay a little mad at him.

"This is so much more fun." He waggled his eyebrows.

"For you maybe."

He clasped her hand and led her toward the dappled gray mare next to his horse.

"Frappe, now you be nice to Madi," he said to the horse, giving her a wink. "She woke up on the wrong side of the bed this morning and is a little grumpy."

Madison narrowed her eyes and growled at him. "I didn't even eat breakfast or take a shower."

"Up you go."

Derin locked his fingers together and crouched slightly to give her a boost.

As if she would give him the satisfaction! Madison grabbed the horn and cantle while placing her foot in the stirrup. She easily pulled herself up into the saddle. No bossy, annoying, handsome cowboy needed.

When she started to turn Frappe away from him, Derin spoke with a slightly patronizing tone.

"Madi."

She glanced over her shoulder.

Derin wiggled a pastry bag in the air. "You wouldn't want to take off without your breakfast."

She leaned down and snatched the breakfast sandwich from his hand.

"Don't think this gets you out of time-out, cowboy."

Derin chuckled as he swung onto his mount. A smile flicked at the corner of her mouth.

"I saw that," he said.

She grumbled as she unwrapped her meal, taking a big bite. The salty bacon combined with the egg and cheese on a fluffy biscuit satiated her quicker than she expected. Guess she was hungrier than she thought.

Derin rode up next to her. "Cole wanted to show his new girlfriend the ranch."

"I heard that! We're just friends," Cole said from behind them.

Madison glanced back at Syd in time to notice the red splotching her freckled cheeks. The way Cole looked at her assistant said he cared for Syd. Good for them. Syd deserved a good guy, and Cole was the real deal.

"Yeah, he's got it bad," Derin teased as he angled toward Madison, hooking a thumb over his shoulder.

She smiled, giving him a knowing look.

"Heard that too. Are you gonna lead this trail ride or just sit around, making jokes at my expense?"

"I was just giving Madi a chance to finish her breakfast."

Madison stuffed the empty wrapper in her pocket. "All done."

"Right this way."

Derin pointed his black stallion toward a pathway covered with pea gravel. It meandered between a few buildings before opening up to reveal a beautiful mountain drenched in gold and rust tones. Her breath lodged in her throat.

"It's beautiful," she whispered.

"It's even prettier at sunrise. But you needed your beauty sleep."

Madison snorted, then flashed a cheeky smile at him.

Her pulse raced as she studied him. So at home on his horse's back. Worn denim. A green and yellow plaid patterned shirt with a white background stretched across his broad back and thick biceps. He wore a dusty brown cowboy hat today. His thick beard covered an angular jaw. Those deep blue eyes sparkled with mischief.

"Careful, Madi. You might make me blush with all your staring."

"I doubt you've ever blushed a day in your life."

"Don't be so sure."

Madison sighed. This man intrigued her and irritated her all at the same time. She thoroughly enjoyed dancing with him last night. She appreciated him taking her on a trail ride, even though he did not give her a heads up. It had been forever since she had ridden. She had forgotten how much she missed it. The smell of leather. The power of the animal beneath her. She breathed deeply of the fresh morning air, feeling the tension leave her body.

Derin shifted in his saddle to look behind him for a few seconds, leather squeaking from the effort.

"Looks like Cole remembered how to ride. Though I think your friend is gonna be sore by the end of the day."

"So am I. It's been a few years."

"Really? Even with you living on a ranch?"

"I haven't been back in ages. And when I am, I don't always have time for a ride."

Derin cleared his throat. "I don't think I could go more than a few days without riding. Djano here about forgot who I was."

"How long has it been?"

He frowned. "Thursday morning. Yesterday was too busy."

She felt a little sorry over the sadness in his tone.

"So why are you working at the sports complex, then?"

Derin flinched. "It's my job. I'm a Vargas and we manage the place."

"But you clearly miss your old job. What was it?"

"Foreman."

She started to press more, but he urged Djano into a trot away from her. Madison couldn't understand why he changed roles if it made him so miserable, and why he kept avoiding questions about it.

# 7

———————

DERIN CLENCHED HIS jaw so tight his teeth hurt. He missed the outdoors, the sunshine overhead, and his powerful horse beneath him. Fresh air and scenic beauty all around him. Cerulean sky overhead. He patted Djano's neck before he slowed him to a walk again.

Madi's question bothered him. He had never been one to shirk his responsibilities. Dalton and Papi expected him to run the sports rehab center, and he would do it. Maybe in time he would come to enjoy it as much as his old job.

"You're grieving." Madi's soft voice startled him. He hadn't noticed her ride up next to him.

"Grieving?"

"Yeah. Any major life change brings some level of grief. We say goodbye to what was. We find a new rhythm and routine. Even when we're excited, there's still a process to let go of the old."

He considered her words. Perhaps he grieved all the things from his old life that he had taken for granted. She might just be on to something.

"You ever miss your home?"

Madi's head turned away from him for a minute.

"Yeah. This ride reminds me how much."

"Tell me about your family's ranch."

"Maybe some other time." She blew out a breath so long

her shoulders sank. "How about one of those one hundred and one questions?"

He chuckled as he swiped to open the app on his phone, glad she embraced the questions.

"How many countries have you been to?"

She puffed her cheeks out. "Woo. Let me think."

He grinned, enjoying how adorable she looked, biting her lip as she mentally tried to count them all.

"Well, having almost achieved a Grand Slam... England, Australia, France. Then I took a trip to Belgium and Germany after the French Open one year. We drove through Luxomberg. How many is that so far?"

"Six. Plus the US makes seven."

"Canada. Oh, yeah. One year on the flight to the UK, we had to stop in Iceland."

Hmm. She had traveled all over the world. He had never even been on an airplane. He drove to California once with his family to see the ocean. And he rode with Papi one year when he purchased a bull from a rancher in Texas.

"That makes nine," she said. "Oh, Mexico too. So, ten."

When she turned those warm brown eyes his way, he swallowed down his embarrassment.

"How about you?"

"One."

She blinked. "Just the US?"

"Yup. Never even flown on a plane."

"You can't be serious! How old are you?"

"Twenty-nine."

"Derin! You've never flown *anywhere*?"

"Nope. Only been to four states. Arizona, California, New Mexico, and Texas."

Madi's eyes rounded. "Really?"

"Honest truth. Think about it. Have your brothers left the ranch much?"

Her face contorted. "I guess not. They flew to watch me

play in New York once."

"Just once, am I right?"

"Yeah."

His stomach tightened. Maybe a man his age should have traveled more than he had.

"Do you ever dream of going somewhere, like for a vacation?"

Derin scoffed. "No vacations on a ranch. You should know that."

"My parents always took time off. At least one week a year. My cousins and uncles came to fill in."

"Don't sound so sad, Madi. I like my life. Don't feel like I'm missing out."

"But do you want to travel somewhere?"

He sighed. "I supposed it would be nice to see the Rockies one day. Maybe some of the national parks."

"That's it?"

"Yeah."

"If you were with someone who traveled, would you just hate it?"

He chuckled at that. "If I was with someone, say you, then I wouldn't mind traveling."

"That's good. I mean, how else would we end up on that deserted island together with a Bible, chocolate, ground coffee for life, Djano, and your hat?"

Derin tossed his head back in laughter. He loved her wit.

"You know, we never determined if that deserted island was tropical or not."

"Is there any other kind?"

Madi shrugged. "Iceland is an island."

"Right. And the Aleutians in Alaska. Probably colder than I'd like to be."

"Did I mention I know how to knit? I'm sure we could find some wild sheep, learn how to spin yarn, and then I'd make you a sweater."

"Without knitting needles?"

"Derin, you underestimate my resourcefulness."

He snorted.

"I would make knitting needles out of some sanded down sticks."

"And where are you getting sandpaper?"

She huffed. "Fine. Tropical island it is. What's your next question?"

"How about we stop and let the greenhorns rest?" He hooked a thumb over his shoulder.

"I could use a break, now that you mention it."

Derin turned Djano toward a picnic area they used on trail rides. When he dismounted, he tied Djano to a hitching post. Madi dismounted and moaned as she gingerly walked toward another hitching post. He grabbed some water and snacks from his saddlebags before placing them on the concrete picnic table.

"Beautiful day," Cole said as he released Sydney's hand, taking a seat at the table next to her.

Derin was happy for his friend. He deserved a good woman, and Sydney seemed like one.

After Madi sat, she snagged his phone.

"Ooo. I like this one. What would your perfect morning look like?"

Derin looped his legs over the bench seat and scooted next to her. "Easy. Riding out toward the horizon on Djano with the sun rising behind me, casting golden rays on Dalton Peak."

Cole laughed. "Sounds like every day of your life."

Derin didn't correct him. It used to be every morning until this year.

"For me," Sydney said, "a perfect morning is one where I can wake up feeling at home. Sunlight streaming through a window, easing me into a quiet day."

"Travel is tough," Cole empathized.

"Yeah. A new place every few weeks. I mean, it's nice to see some of the world, but I don't have a place of my own. When we break, I go to my parents—to the room I grew up in. Even that doesn't feel like home."

"I hear ya." Cole reached over and held her hand.

"What about you, Madison?" Sydney asked.

Derin watched Madi. Her eyes seemed to stare off to some place far away.

"My perfect morning? Waking up next to my husband on a day with no agenda. Kids piling on top of us. Tickles and giggles." She let out a soft breath, rubbing her hands on her legs. "Guess it'll be a while."

"Sounds lovely. I might have to borrow your dream morning." Sydney offered a sweet smile.

Derin thought he might just like to be the husband Madi woke up beside.

MADISON TOOK A long swig of her water, kicking herself for sharing that. At least no one mistook it as flirting with Derin. She meant what she said—waking up next to a husband with her joyful children giggling as they jumped in bed and snuggled with them.

How many times had she and her brothers done that with her parents? Not enough. Some of her best memories were of that time. Her parents showered love and attention on each of them. No urgency to rush off to their day. Those were special mornings. Something she longed to recreate.

Yet, her pro tennis career took her far away from any chance of marriage and a family of her own. Her eyes burned, and she stood, hoping no one noticed.

She walked over to Frappe, running her hand along the mare's velvety face. *Lord, why are these dreams and desires com-*

*ing to the surface now? Are you trying to tell me something?*

A breeze tickled the fine hairs on her neck. Maybe her pro tennis career was ending. Maybe she stood on the brink of those dreams coming true. No more travel. Living a settled life. Marrying and starting a family.

Madison rested her forehead against Frappe's. The horse pressed against her, seeming to offer her comfort.

For the hundredth time since the Open, she wondered what her life would look like without tennis. What would she do for work? Help on a ranch? Coach young athletes? Something she had yet to discover?

She had no college education. After high school, she went to the Olympics and right into pro tennis. Maybe she should have been taking online classes the last few years. At least then she would have a degree to fall back on.

When she tried to picture anything beyond the charity tournament in six weeks, she could see nothing clearly.

"Where did you go?"

Derin's husky voice stirred her from her spiraling thoughts.

"Ready?" she asked as she turned to face him.

"You okay?"

Madison forced a smile to her lips. "Yeah. I'm great."

A shadow fell over his features as he studied her face. She told herself not to look away. At last, his face relaxed.

"They want to head back. Cole thinks he can find the way, but I should probably lead them."

"Oh, good. I'm fine if we head back."

She tried to lighten her mood with a self-deprecating laugh. "I'm not used to riding anymore."

"We could change that."

She expelled a loud breath. "I need to focus on tennis right now. This has been nice. Thanks for bringing me."

He grinned and handed her his phone. "Queue up the next question while I pack up."

"Bossy much?"

He chuckled. "You know you like me just the way I am."

Madison watched him walk away all full of swagger. Yeah, she did like him just as he was—manly, confident, and surprisingly caring.

She stuffed his phone in her other back pocket before mounting Frappe. Then she retrieved it and picked the next question. As soon as he rode up next to her, she handed him the phone.

"Ready, cowboy?"

"Shoot."

"Do you prefer working as part of a team or alone?"

"Team. One hundred percent. As the foreman, the tough decisions were mine, but I always listened to the men and their ideas. Sometimes they had better ones than mine. Even though I might ride for hours too far away from the others for casual conversation, I still felt like we were a team. And, of course, vaccinating the cattle is a team sport. It takes every man doing his part to make it happen."

"Hmm. I can see why this new role is uncomfortable. You're still gathering your team."

Derin frowned. "What do you mean?"

"Well, you've got Cole. And Ryan and Hudson. Yet, you still need a few more people and you all haven't had time to gel."

He tilted his head to the side. "I suppose you're right. What about you?"

"Tennis isn't exactly a team sport."

"Yeah, but the question is about what you prefer."

Madison's shoulders sagged. "I guess I like both. There are times it brings me tremendous satisfaction knowing I've accomplished something on my own. Like winning a tournament. Other times, I see how I am part of a team. Coach Layla, Kevin, my manager, and Syd. Without them, I wouldn't be where I am today."

"See, you're more of a team player than you thought."

"Huh. I guess so."

Silence settled between them for the rest of the ride back to the ranch. When they reined in at the stables, Derin volunteered to care for all the horses. Madison waved off his help. She could groom Frappe. Besides, she kinda liked the mare.

Cole hesitated, and Derin insisted he walk Sydney back to the casita.

"He needs more practice with the horses, but didn't seem right to keep him from his girl."

Madison laughed. "Sydney is his girl now?"

"Duh."

She accepted the brush he handed her. "What will she do if I retire?"

"So you're thinking about it?"

Madison ran the brush along Frappe's dappled coat. Such pretty spotted coloring.

"I might not have a choice, Derin. I don't want to give up tennis. I love it."

She finished one side and circled to the other, using long, gentle strokes over the mare's coat.

"Yet, if my game play doesn't improve from practice yesterday... If the pain doesn't stop coming back..."

He cleared his throat. "I get it, Madi. Just don't get so stuck in your head that you cause yourself to perform poorly."

She snorted. "That's almost exactly what Layla said yesterday."

"I've played enough sports, and watched 'em too, to know that most of the battle is in the mind. Where your thoughts go, there your flesh follows."

The odd word choice gave her pause. She sensed Derin was no longer talking about sports. Perhaps some personal struggle of his own. She shrugged off the thoughts as she finished grooming Frappe.

Derin's brother, Dylan, came by and offered to turn out the horses. Madison relinquished the lead. Then she walked outside of the stables.

"Well, thanks for the ride. I'm off for a nice hot shower and maybe some lunch."

"You want me to drive you home?"

"Naw. I'd like to walk. Not that far, and I could use the time to pray."

"See you around."

She waved before he hopped into his truck. Then she strolled along the path to the casita, thanking God for the beautiful day.

Despite having no clear direction yet, she felt His peace. She knew God was with her, no matter what happened. Eventually, she would figure out her next steps.

# 8

---

"HERC MALVOY IS all settled."

Derin looked up from his computer at the sound of Cole's voice from the doorway. He rubbed his thumb and index finger over his eyes. "What room is he in?"

"He booked the rust-colored family casita."

"Sedona Casita."

"Yeah, that's the one."

"Did he bring family with him?"

"His wife and twin girls. They are adorable. You can tell he loves them."

Derin nodded, weary of sitting at his desk.

"He loves the facilities. Already started spreading the word to his team."

"That's good."

"Anyway, I was gonna grab some supper in the dining hall before Bible study. You coming tonight."

"Yeah, I'll be along soon."

Cole turned and left.

Derin let out a long breath as he powered off his computer. A month into his new gig, and he still felt off most days. At least he didn't have a potential career-ending injury to deal with, like many of their clients, like Hercules Malvoy.

The all-pro tight end started the season with a torn Achilles in his first game. Herc played for the pro football team in Dallas and still had three years left on his contract. At twenty-nine—same age as Derin—he faced the strong possibility of being cut and losing his livelihood.

Such thoughts made Derin twice as grateful for his family's business. He would always have a job, even if it wasn't his ideal one.

He snagged his hat from its hook by the door and headed out to his truck. Then he drove over to the dining hall.

The buzz of conversation comforted him as he stepped into the large room. Guests sat around tables enjoying Chef's delicious food. He ambled toward the back of the line, only a few people deep. Good. He needed to hurry if he planned to make it to the Bible study on time.

He took one of the to-go containers, piling it full of fried pork chops, scalloped potatoes, and three biscuits. After grabbing a few pats of foil-wrapped butter and some plastic ware, he filled a styrofoam cup with ice and soda. Then he drove over to the bunkhouse.

"Hey, Derin!" his youngest brother, Drake, greeted him. "It's still weird not seeing you here every night."

Derin side hugged his little brother. "You saying you miss me?"

"Like an extra hole in my head."

His other younger brother, Devon, gave him a man hug before finding a spot on the couch. Parker Quaid, a wrangler, nodded a greeting, as did Adan Franco, the study leader. Even Dylan showed up. First time since he had married Adan's little sister. He had become an instant father to Brisa's wheelchair-bound boy Braden. Derin loved that kid's joy.

After Adan opened in prayer, Derin scarfed down his meal so he could take part in the discussion.

Dalton arrived, apologizing for being late.

"Padre isn't feeling well, so Papi isn't coming."

Derin frowned, concerned about his grandfather.

"What's wrong?"

"He was in a lot of pain. Kept saying it was just arthritis and the cold weather, but Papi didn't want to leave Mami alone to deal with him."

Parker snorted. "This ain't cold. Flagstaff is cold. Mom said it snowed up there today."

Dalton hitched a shoulder. "Adan, sorry for the interruption."

"Cole, would you mind reading James 4:6-10?" Adan asked.

"Sure."

Derin tapped on his phone until he found the passage on his Bible app. Cole flipped there in a well-worn paper Bible, with lots of notes in the margin. No one could ever accuse his friend of not being devout. His Bible and his life proved his seriousness. It inspired Derin to want to be better.

"Therefore it says, 'God opposes the proud but gives grace to the humble.' Submit yourselves therefore to God. Resist the devil, and he will flee from you. Draw near to God, and he will draw near to you. Cleanse your hands, you sinners, and purify your hearts, you double-minded. Be wretched and mourn and weep. Let your laughter be turned to mourning and your joy to gloom. Humble yourselves before the Lord, and he will exalt you."

Derin rubbed a hand over his heart as the words hit him hard. There were so many layers to that passage to unpack. On one hand, he felt relieved that resisting the devil would cause him to flee. That's what he was trying to do. Move closer to God and stop living like he had for the last decade plus of his life. He had seen the fruit of his recent choices even in his relationship with Madi.

She was the first and only woman he ever bothered to get to know. The only one where he had shown restraint despite a sizzling attraction.

Yet there were several warnings in that passage for him.

He should not become arrogant about his success. That would lead him to take pride in himself. He still needed to submit and be humble before God and others.

Derin shifted in his seat as he closed the lid on his empty meal container. *Be wretched and mourn and weep. Let your laughter be turned to mourning and your joy to gloom.* What did that mean? Maybe Adan would explain it to them.

Adan looked at each man in the room as he spoke. "Just before this passage, James admonishes believers not to be worldly. He says our passions are at war within us—that friendship with the world puts us in opposition to God."

Derin's heart squeezed tight. All those years he sought worldly pleasure, self-gratification, over choosing God. He had opposed God.

He swallowed down the lump in his throat as remorse overwhelmed him. Pride had blinded him to the truth—living like that actually *hurt* him. He had damaged himself. Derin looked down at his hands. Hands that had embraced lust and sin.

Suddenly, the verse about turning laughter into mourning and joy into gloom made complete sense. He had laughed and acted downright joyful about sleeping with any woman that would have him. A heart filled with pride. Now, as he humbled himself, yet again, his heart mourned. He wanted to weep over his wretchedness.

His reason for his abrupt end to his former ways had more to do with his own shock over how many lines he had crossed that he swore he never would. It hadn't been conviction. The last nine months Derin had been white-knuckling his way to *behavior* change.

God wanted his heart, his humble posture, not someone who acted his way into some moral standard of goodness.

Derin propped his elbows on the table and dropped his head into his hands. The first sob wrested from his throat, mortifying him—probably shocking every man in the room.

The tears, as ugly and wretched as he, flowed freely. He wanted to give all of his heart to God. He no longer wanted to oppose the Creator of the universe. Derin wanted to honor God in his thoughts. He wanted the next woman he slept with to be his wife on their wedding night. No more flirting with fire. No more pride.

Dylan was the first to lay a hand on his shoulder. He only knew it by recognizing his brother's boots, which popped into his line of sight as he stared at the floor. Then another hand until the room full of men placed hands on his back and whispered words over him. He felt God's presence as he poured his heart out to the One who made him.

*From this day forward, Lord, I want to be in lockstep with You and not opposition. I want what You want. I want what Your word says. This is my heart. Take it all. No matter how painful. No matter how long it takes to root out the deeply entrenched weeds in it. I am Yours. Fully. Show me the way forward.*

The words of his soul faded quickly, followed by the tears. Derin lifted his head and swiped the back of his hand over his damp eyes. Hands fell away. Dylan squeezed his shoulder and made eye contact. Then he nodded as if he knew exactly what had happened inside of Derin.

Even though these men weren't part of his support group, they were his brothers and friends. They had seen his behavior change and probably guessed something had stirred inside of him. He wasn't the first in the study to surrender to some Spirit-led nudge. He wouldn't be the last.

Adan held his gaze for a minute. Derin nodded, giving him permission to continue. He appreciated it. He listened throughout the rest of the study.

When it finished, he shot to his feet and hurried from the building.

"Der!" Dylan jogged after him. "Do you want to talk?"

He turned toward his brother. "Not tonight, Dyl. Thanks."

"I'll keep praying for you."

Derin gave one sharp nod before climbing behind the wheel of his big truck. Maybe some day he would tell his brothers what happened. Not then. It still felt too raw, and he needed it to stay between him and God.

A FEW DAYS before the mock tournament, Madison woke with piercing pain shooting down her arm. Her shoulder burned and her fingers felt numb. Had she slept on it wrong?

As she showered and dressed for the day, she noticed her reduced mobility. She headed over to the sports complex and found Ryan in his office.

"Madison, what brings you over?"

She swallowed down the fear and the emotion it brought to the surface.

"My shoulder. Something isn't right."

"Pain?"

She tucked her lip under her teeth, willing the burning in her eyes not to overflow.

"Okay. Let's look."

Madison sat on the edge of his exam table and removed her tank top, knowing her sports bra provided enough modesty. Ryan's hands felt like ice against her skin, causing her to jump.

"The heat is radiating off your shoulder. When is the last time you iced?"

"After my shower this morning. About an hour ago."

Ryan asked her to lie face down on the table, which had a special face rest. She couldn't see his face and the time that lapsed made her anxiety rise.

"I'm gonna put some anti-inflammatory topical cream

on it."

She heard a drawer slide open, then closed. Ryan explained what he was doing as he applied the cream. Then he placed a towel over her skin before putting a large ice pack on it.

"Did you strain it yesterday?"

"No. Just a normal practice."

"Hmm. I'm gonna call your coach. I'll be back in twenty minutes to remove the ice."

"Okay."

She heard his footsteps fade. Ugh. Madison hated the waiting, especially when all she could do was think about her injury.

A few minutes passed before a familiar voice greeted her.

"Madi, Ryan said you're having pain."

Derin. The one person she most wanted to see. Or hear.

"Yeah. I woke up with shooting pain down my arm. Nerve pain."

"You want me to get our orthopedic surgeon in here? Have her examine it?"

"I…"

The fear choked off her words. A warm hand clasped hers as the sound of a chair scraping across the tile floor echoed in the room.

"I'm right here, Madi."

"What if—"

"You know better than to go there. Who, by worrying, can add a single hour to her life, Madi?"

She expelled a loud breath. "You're right. Yeah, could you call the orthopedic surgeon? Just to be sure."

The sound of his phone dialing faded. She tried to wait patiently as Derin spoke with the doctor's office.

"She'll be here in thirty."

"Thank you, Derin."

"Want me to wait with you?"

Madison worried she was monopolizing his time. Surely, he had important work to do. At last, she answered, "I'm sure you're busy."

"Not too busy to wait with you."

"Okay."

A few minutes later, Ryan removed the ice and helped her sit up. Then he left to work with one of the many other athletes staying there.

Derin offered her a sweet smile. "Could be nothing. Just inflammation, you know."

Tears pooled in the corner of her eyes, spilling over in rivulets down her cheeks. Derin rubbed his thumb over one cheek. Then he sat on the table next to her, looping his arm around her. Madison snuggled against his side, resting her head over his heart.

In the weeks since the horse ride, they spent some evenings at the dining hall together. Once they drove into town for a meal. Sometimes he came over and sat on the front porch with her. They continued working their way through the one hundred and one questions.

The more Madison learned about him, the more she liked him. Neither had been eager to define their relationship as anything serious.

In moments like then, waiting for the orthopedic surgeon, it felt like he was her boyfriend. Attentive. Comforting. Invested in her well-being.

"Madison?" A short woman approached with hand outstretched. "I'm Dr. Amy Stone."

Madison shook her hand. As Derin scooted off the table, the scuffing sound of his rough denim against the leather table echoed in the room. Madison answered all of Dr. Stone's questions. Dr. Stone examined her shoulder and arm. Then she held Madison's arm and rotated it in a few different directions, studying her shoulder's flexibility.

"Well, I think it's very inflamed. I can give you a cortisone shot to help reduce it quickly. And we can get Ryan to work your shoulder with some gentle exercises."

"Okay. Let's do it."

"I recommend taking a day or two off from practice, too."

Madison flashed a frown at Derin. "The mock tournament is in three days. I need the practice."

Dr. Stone tapped some notes into her phone. "If the inflammation and pain subside, then you should be fine to play. If not, I wouldn't recommend it."

After Dr. Stone administered the cortisone, Ryan came in for the exercises Dr. Stone ordered.

"Madi." Derin stood and tapped his fisted hand lightly against the side of his leg. "Will you be okay? I need to..."

"Thanks for sticking around as long as you did. I really appreciate it."

"Talk later."

He flashed a soft smile before he left.

"You two dating?" Ryan asked as he rubbed his thumb over her trapezius muscle.

"No."

Ryan snorted. "If you say so."

Ryan dug into her rhomboid close to her surgery site. When Madison sucked in a sharp breath, he eased off the pressure.

"He really likes you."

Madison frowned, but remained silent. She liked Derin. Enjoyed his company and she would have to be blind not to notice the chemistry between them.

Except she didn't have time for romance. She had a tournament to win and a career to save. No matter how much she enjoyed spending time with Derin Vargas, she couldn't afford any distractions. They were just friends. She would make sure they stayed that way.

# 9

---

THE MORNING OF the mock tournament, Madison woke early, slow to get out of bed. Instead, she prayed before moving a muscle. *Lord, I want to beg You for healing. I want to keep playing tennis. Yet, I know I can trust Your plan for me — even if it isn't what I want. If it is time for my career to come to a close, give me the strength to accept it.*

She rubbed her hands over her face. Then she eased onto her side and pushed up from the bed with her good arm. She rotated her shoulder and ran through the exercises Ryan recommended. Her shoulder felt better than it had in a few days. Maybe Layla would clear her to play in the mock tournament.

After she showered and donned her white tennis dress, Madison walked over to the tennis court with her gym bag and racket. The tournament wouldn't start for a few hours yet. She walked the perimeter of the court with earbuds in and music playing. She visualized her first match. Serve. Groundstroke. Overhead smash. Two-handed backhand. Forehand volley. She walked through each stroke as if she held her racket, allowing muscle memory to dictate her motion.

To an outsider, her mental warm up might seem odd. She probably looked like she danced to the music in her mind, fluid movements melding one into the other. She ran through the steps four times before she walked away from the court.

Madison resisted the anxiety that threatened to consume her. She let her music drown out the lie that she could never be good enough again. Though it may be true, she refused to believe it yet. She was still recovering. Still hoped.

As she lifted her gaze, slowly returning to the real world, she noticed Syd working alongside Drake Vargas and several others. They set up tables along the gravel pathway around the tennis courts. After lining each with tablecloths, a few cowboys raised pop-up shades over each. The chef and restaurant staff began filling the tables with snacks, food, and beverages.

Madison wondered how big of a crowd they expected for the mock tournament.

A hand tapped her shoulder, and she squealed. As she turned, Layla apologized.

"You ready to play today?"

"I think so."

"After the first match, if you're in pain, we can pull you. The other players won't mind."

"My stamina for a tournament is waning. I need the practice. I think I'll be fine."

Layla studied her for a minute. "Alright. We'll let you go the whole day and deal with the fallout later."

Madison thanked her.

A half hour later, the players arrived. Madison warmed up with Bella. They stretched and caught up on the latest news about Bella's family. Before she knew it, the tournament official, Cole Gregory, announced the first set of match ups.

"Bella Gaines and Madison Moore. Court 1."

Madison headed to the court beside her friend. A referee introduced himself. Madison and Bella met on opposite sides of the net, shaking hands. Then it was go time.

"You got this, Madi!"

A smile tilted the corner of her mouth at Derin's boisterous cheer. She widened her stance, twirled her racket, and crouched slightly, ready to receive Bella's serve. A forehand volley. Backhand stroke. Then came the perfect opportunity for an overhead smash. The ball hit the court hard on Bella's side before bouncing above her reach.

Perfect!

As the match continued, Madison's confidence grew. Her shoulder felt good, even though some stiffness warned her she still wasn't one hundred percent yet.

When the match ended, Madison won, but not by much. Still, a win was a win.

"Good game, Gaines."

"You looked great Madison. Good form. Best I've seen you play since your surgery."

Madison hugged Bella, thanking her for the kind words. Then she walked over to her gym bag before wiping the sweat from her face with a towel.

When she noticed Derin in the crowd, he gave her two thumbs up. She responded with a smile and a brief nod. Then she downed some water.

For her second match, she faced off with another top-notch singles player. They drew court 1, so Madison took the side opposite from the one she played on earlier.

Her first serve immediately felt off. Ripples of pain shot through her shoulder, fading to a dull ache. Though she returned most of the balls during the first half of the match, the second half wore her out. The longer the match went, the worse she played.

Periodically, she heard encouragement from Derin and Bella. It made little difference. The pain shot down to her hand, leaving a trail of numbness behind. Instead of returning the ball with a forehand stroke, the racket slipped from her loose fingers, clattering to the court.

Madison swooped down to pick it up. Catching her lower lip between her teeth, she bit back a moan.

As the match came to a close, she had visions of standing in front of a podium announcing her retirement. She thanked her opponent for a good game. Her opponent offered words of compassion. Madison let them bounce off her back as a tear dripped down the side of her face.

She iced her shoulder for a few minutes before the third match. In the end, it made no difference. Her shoulder ached, nearly as bad as before the surgery. Though scheduled for a fourth match, Madison quit after the third.

When she reached down for her gym bag, heat warmed her cheeks. She stormed from the court, dejected. Everyone would know soon enough that her career was over. She just needed to admit it to herself first.

DERIN STOOD IN line for a hot dog and soda at the shaded food tables after Madi's second match. He noticed the moment she gave up. He saw the fine lines etched near the corner of her eyes from the pain.

He wished he could carry some of this for her. Except it wasn't his burden to bear.

After paying for his hot dog, despite Drake telling him he didn't need to, Derin dressed it with just about everything. Ketchup, mustard, relish, chili, jalapenos, onion, and cheese. A smile twitched on his lips. His brothers always teased him about his choice of condiments. Most of them chose chili, jalapenos, onions, and cheese. Though Devon preferred the more traditional ketchup, mustard, and relish toppings. Derin loved it piled with everything.

As he bit off a huge chunk of his hot dog, he scanned the crowd for Madison. She still had two more matches to play—if she made it through the whole day. Her coach approached her. The two spoke as Derin stood too far away to hear it. He chomped up the rest of the hot dog and downed his soda before taking a seat in the temporary bleachers for Madi's third match.

He watched with bated breath as Madi tossed the bright yellow ball in the air and brought her racket down hard against it. It flew across the court, but his eyes didn't follow the ball. He noticed her wince.

When her opponent sent the ball low, she tried for a single-handed backhand. The racket dropped from her hand, bouncing to the ground. The entire crowd went silent with a collective gasp. Madi's expression tightened.

Derin knew she felt pain—could tell it from her stiff posture and scowl. His heart ached for her.

He had known plenty of physical pain in his time. Once a bull kicked him hard in the thigh, ripping his jeans open and gashing his skin. Thirteen stitches later and with a deep purple bruise, he limped around the ranch for a week. Hurt like the dickens when he smashed the same spot against a fence post a few days later.

That sharp hissing intake of air that he had made, that's what Madi's face looked like. Each volley and stroke ripped another piece of her confidence away, adding mental pain to the physical.

At the end of the third match, he noticed her red eyes and damp cheeks as she stalked off the court. He bolted to his feet, following her as she scurried to the sports complex.

She shoved the glass doors open hard with her good arm. They eased shut before he caught up. Once inside the building, his eyes adjusted to the lower light. He glimpsed her blond ponytail just before she ducked into the women's locker room.

Derin paused. Probably wasn't a good idea for the CEO of Vargas Sports to follow a woman in there. He eased closer to the door. It opened, and a brunette nodded at him.

"Anyone else in there?"

"Just Madison Moore."

"Thanks."

He shoved the door open, and in two strides swept his Madi off the bench. He held her in his arms, rubbing circles on her back. Her tears soaked through his polo shirt, which he still hated wearing.

She sniffed and leaned back.

"It's over, Derin." Madi's voice croaked, causing his protectiveness to surface.

"I don't think so. Not yet."

"How can you say that? Didn't you see how pitiful I played? I dropped my racket!"

He released her as she stepped away from him.

"I saw a strong woman athlete who is barely out of rehab from shoulder surgery. Your first match, you nailed it. Second one, I could tell you were in pain. Probably should have rested at that point."

"How can I remain on the pro tours if I can't even make it through two matches, much less three?"

"There's still time to build your stamina."

The door opened, and Derin heard a woman gasp. He apologized and guided Madi out of the locker room to the privacy of his office.

"It's not over yet," he said as he offered her one of the guest seats. The other shiny leather seat groaned as he plopped onto it.

"It is. I'm just too stubborn to admit it."

"No. Right now, you're letting one terrible match dictate your future. I don't think you've tried hard enough yet."

Madi folded her arms around her middle. "I'm a realist, Derin. It's over."

Derin leaned forward. "Look at me, Madi."

When she did, he continued. "Rest your shoulder for a

few days. Ice it. Then practice for the charity tournament. You still have a few weeks."

She expelled a slow breath while uncrossing her arms. "Fine."

"It's not over yet. Your body is still healing." He lifted his hand to her cheek and brushed away her tears, wishing he could give her some of his strength.

"Right. You're right."

Madi straightened her back. Then she rubbed her hands along her thighs.

"I should go ice my shoulder."

"Need help?"

"No. I'll head back to the casita. I've got my sling ice pack."

Derin stood with her. Then he held the door for her and watched her walk away.

*Lord, please help Madi. Heal her body. Help her not to give up yet.*

His own words pierced his heart. Giving up on his CEO job crossed his mind more than once over the past few days. It was hard work—not physically. Mentally.

He and Cole spent hours on a schedule for Ryan and Hudson, staggering the eight clients. It had been hard figuring out how to balance all the demands of each athlete. Most of them needed to work with both Ryan and Hudson.

Then he sat in front of his computer, researching recommendations for group counseling for athletes recovering from potential career-ending injuries. He thought they might need to hire a part-time counselor, so he also researched salaries and contacts in the area.

After several long days with no obvious answers, Derin felt discouraged and worried for the hundredth time if he was the wrong choice for the CEO.

So, yeah, he had his doubts about his own future. He and Madi both needed to fight the battles in their minds. He had to stop whining in his about all the things he missed about being the foreman.

Instead, he ought to embrace his new role. He enjoyed meeting new clients. After several tours this week, he had refined his speech. He pointed out all the great facilities, introduced them to Hudson and Ryan, reassured their fears. Prayed for them. One man he prayed for in the moment — something he had never done before. Others he prayed for as they came to mind.

As CEO, Derin made a difference in the lives of these athletes — people afraid of the future. They didn't know if they would still have a job in a few months. They needed hope. Hope just like he found in the love of God — a God who never gave up on him, even when he failed so horribly.

An idea formed at the recesses of his mind. Maybe they should offer more than a support group alone. A Bible study, prayer, and counseling. Hearing from other athletes who overcame. And hearing from some who hadn't. They needed to know life on the other side of physical rehab could be just as fulfilling as their lives had been, even if it looked different from their life before.

And Madison Moore was the first athlete he needed to convince.

# 10

A WEEK AFTER the mock tournament, Madison felt low. She could not escape the feeling that her pro tennis career was over. Her shoulder ached constantly. Physical therapy helped some. Another cortisone shot did too. Neither of those were long-term solutions for her broken body.

Walking back from her latest round of PT, she scuffed her feet along the path. The sun warmed her tanned skin and the fresh air filled her lungs. A noise from the arena caught her attention, so she ambled that direction. When she entered, the smell of hay and horse hung heavy in the air. The sound of laughter and joy drew her deeper into the building.

Several children of varying ages waited by the perimeter of the arena. Giggles brought a smile to her face until she realized all the children sat in wheelchairs. Madison's heart squeezed in her chest.

A brunette led a very calm horse to a platform while Derin's brother, Dylan, she thought, wheeled a young boy to a lift that raised his chair to the top of the platform. Dylan said something to the boy, and a grin lit his face. She watched as the muscular man settled the child onto the horse's back in a specialized saddle. Then the brunette led the horse away from the platform. She handed the reins to the little boy but kept pace with the slow walk of the horse.

"Look, Daddy! I'm riding!"

"I see you, son."

Madison's breath caught in her throat as she realized the little boy was Derin's nephew. Her eyes burned as she witnessed the pure look of love on Dylan's face. His son's determined expression endeared him to her.

As she struggled to get her emotions under control, her mind raced. This father and son had something to truly be sad about — the loss of the little boy's mobility. Yet amid everything, they found such deep joy. They didn't let his disability stop him from doing something he clearly loved.

She had nothing to complain about. She had a wonderful run playing pro tennis. Even if she could no longer play professionally, she could play for the joy of it. The Lord would provide for her. She could learn other ways of earning an income. Or she could go home and contribute to the success of her family's ranch.

"Miss! Miss!"

Madison turned to look at the little girl with happy eyes. Realizing she called to her, Madison strode over to her.

"Can you help me?"

"Sure, sweetie. What do you need?"

"I can't get this helmet fastened and my turn is next."

Madison crouched down to the girl's level. The helmet rested snuggly on the little girl's head. Madison took the two ends of the loose straps and snicked them together before adjusting the straps to remove any slack. It was then she noticed the hook over the stub of the little girl's arm. She had one full leg and one stump, one full arm and one stump.

"Thanks!" The little girl squeezed Madison's hand with her good one before she wheeled herself over to the gate.

"They are resilient kids," a man's voice came from her right. He introduced himself as Adan Franco. She introduced herself as well.

"The little boy is my nephew, Braden."

"He seems so happy. And his dad is practically bursting his buttons."

"Step-dad."

Madison turned her head toward Adan with an eyebrow lifted.

"He lost his biological father and his legs in an accident over a year ago. My sister came back home and my best friend, Dylan, married her. He's in the process of adopting Braden as his son."

"Oh, wow."

"That little girl, Cadence, she lost her limbs in an accident on her family's ranch. She had been playing with some dangerous equipment. By the time her father reached her, it was too late to save her limbs. She doesn't remember the accident."

"That's probably a good thing."

"Yeah."

"They all seem so happy."

Adan chuckled. "That's what Braden's Hope is all about. Equine therapy to help hurting hearts and challenged bodies find their joy."

"Hmm. Seems like equine therapy could help the rehabbing athletes find their joy, too."

"You know, you might be on to something, Madison."

Warmth and peace filled her soul as she continued to watch the children ride horses. Some had been riding for a while, easily directing the horse with their legs or stumps and the reins. Others appeared new, still learning how to work with the horse.

"Adan, what if Derin made helping the kids part of the schedule for the sports complex clients?"

Adan rubbed a hand over his chin. "I think both the kids and athletes would enjoy it."

"It would help the clients gain a proper perspective of their trials. It did for me."

"I love your idea. I'll have Shannon Burke—she runs the charity—contact him."

"Would you mind if I told him about it first?"

"Certainly. I'll let her know to expect a visit from Derin soon. She works out of an office by the resort reception area."

"Thanks, Adan. Seems like you all are doing great work here."

"We are."

Madison turned away to the sounds of laughter and joy, allowing it to bolster her hurting heart. No matter what happened with her career, she would be just fine.

DERIN DUCKED INTO the shadows when he noticed Madison talking with Adan, a pinch of jealousy rising in his chest. Her face appeared brighter than he had seen it in weeks. Not since line dancing with her. Maybe on the horse ride. He hoped the handsome former pro bull rider wasn't the reason for it.

When she left the arena, Derin strode toward Adan.

"Uncle Adan! Uncle Derin! Did you see me? I rode by myself!"

Adan laughed. "I saw you, cowpoke." Then to Derin, he added, "Don't worry. Loretta walked beside him. He's not quite ready for a solo ride without close supervision."

"Still, that's quite an accomplishment for only three months."

"Yeah." Adan's chest puffed.

Derin understood the feeling. Though Braden was his nephew by marriage, he loved the kid as if he were blood. Kinda made him long for a few kids of his own.

Dylan reached down and lifted his almost-son into his

arms, hugging him for several seconds, whispering words of praise. Then he settled him into his chair and used the lift to lower him to the ground. As soon as he cleared the lift, Braden wheeled quickly toward them, Dylan jogging up behind him.

"It was so much fun!"

Derin ruffled Braden's hair and crouched in front of him. "I know what you mean. I love riding. Can't wait until we can go on a trail ride together, buddy."

"Me either!"

A grin split the kid's face, causing Derin's heart to float. Crazy that he could love the little bug so much already.

Adan walked next to a chattering Braden as they moved to watch the other riders, leaving Dylan and Derin standing side-by-side.

"How are you and Madison?" Dylan asked in his soft voice.

Derin lifted his cowboy hat and ran a hand through his hair before plopping it down again.

"Good."

"Keeping it..." Dylan's face twitched. "Pure?"

"Yeah."

Derin figured his older brother had guessed his struggle. Kinda hard not to notice when your brother goes out every weekend night for years, then suddenly stops.

"Still praying for you."

"Thanks, Dyl." He cleared his throat. "Seems like married life is treating you well."

Dylan grinned. "Yeah. Brisa and Braden are wonderful."

Derin slapped a hand on his shoulder. "It's only been two months. I think that qualifies as the honeymoon stage."

"My feelings for them won't change—except to grow deeper."

Derin squeezed Dylan's shoulder before releasing it. "I know."

"I saw Madison earlier. Did she take off?"

Derin nodded.

"What brings you by?"

"Just hoping for a glimpse of the equine therapy session. Always puts life in perspective."

Dylan agreed.

"Well, I better get back to work."

"Hey, Der. That tournament turned out great. Rennie said bookings for sports clients increased as a result."

He already knew that. Surprised him that Dylan cared. Though he supposed it shouldn't. Dylan had always been very supportive.

"Yeah. Cole and I need to firm up the program."

"You'll figure it out. Never seen you stuck on a problem for long."

"Thanks, bro."

Dylan headed toward his best friend and his son. Derin watched them for another minute. His brother was an excellent dad.

Derin's mind snagged on that thought. Would he be a great dad, too? Or would his short-comings haunt him forever?

He stuffed away the doubt as he walked out of the arena toward his waiting truck. He sat in it and texted Cole, asking him to invite Sydney to dinner at their place. Then he texted Madi.

Her response came quickly: *I'd love to have dinner at your place. Double date sounds nice.*

A smile spread across his face as he drove over to the dining hall. He spoke with Drake and ordered the meal before returning to his office to finish his day.

At five-thirty, he picked up the meal from the dining hall. Then he drove home, since Cole volunteered to pick up the girls. Derin wasn't sure the three of them would fit in the McLaren, but Cole would know best.

He set plates on the table that neither he nor Cole had used for eating since they grabbed takeout from the dining hall most days. Then he placed the silverware next to each plate. He scrounged around the cupboards for four matching glasses, relieved when he found enough. After brewing iced tea, he placed the pitcher in the fridge.

Ugh. Dessert.

Derin texted his mami. She responded she would bring something by around six-thirty. She promised not to be too nosy. He snorted. Like that would happen.

He glanced at the time and spritzed on a little cologne. It was hard to get out of the mindset of showering before a meal. Sitting behind his desk for his job made it unnecessary.

A few minutes later, the sporty growl of Cole's car silenced. Laughter came from the front porch. Derin swung the door open for the ladies.

"I can't believe we squeezed both of us in that seat!" Madi exclaimed.

"Cole, you may need to buy a car with more than two seats," Sydney teased.

Cole laughed. "When the time is right, I'll buy a second car."

Derin's mouth went dry and words evaporated from his mind as his gaze snagged on Madi. She looked gorgeous. She wore a teal sleeveless sundress that hugged her curves before flaring at the waist. Her long, muscular legs looked silky. Derin's eyes shifted back to her face quickly as heat warmed his face. Her long blond hair hung around her shoulders in beachy waves. The subtle hint of makeup made her face glow. And those luscious lips. So inviting.

"You gonna invite us in, cowboy?" she teased.

Derin stepped aside and motioned for them to enter with the sweep of his hand, still unable to speak.

"Do we get the grand tour first?" Sydney asked.

Cole showed them around while Derin tried to get his

brain restarted. He went to the kitchen and opened the containers of food, setting them on the table, thankful Drake had packaged the food to be served family style instead of Derin's usual single meal container.

"Looks like a bachelor pad," Madi teased as she stood by the table. "Any seating order?"

Derin quickly moved to her side and held a chair for her. He kissed her cheek before she sat, whispering, "You look stunning."

The pink on her cheeks deepened, causing warmth to spread through him. When Sydney sat, both Derin and Cole took their seats on the opposite ends of the table. It felt right having them there. So homey.

MADISON ALLOWED HERSELF to smile as she bowed her head for Cole's blessing. She had left Derin Vargas speechless when she entered his home. She hadn't tried too hard to dress up after receiving his dinner invitation.

Okay, so maybe she had. Curling her hair. Dusting on some makeup. A little lotion on her legs. She had expected him to appreciate the extra work. Speechless, though, had not been her goal. Clearly, the cowboy liked her.

Madison inwardly rolled her eyes at herself. It's not like she didn't know that from all their other interactions. She liked him, too. Felt a deep connection building between them. More than just chemistry.

"Smells delicious," she said, forcing her thoughts back to the meal.

"Maybe next time, we can grill out. I just didn't have any food on hand."

"Do either of you cook?" Sydney asked.

Cole snorted. "A little."

"Same. Between Mami's amazing meals and food at the dining hall, never had to." Derin shrugged. "Learned how to grill a few things from Mateo, our old foreman."

"Either of you cook?" Cole asked.

Sydney blushed. "I can manage when needed. My mom taught me the basics."

Derin looked at Madison, and her cheeks warmed under his questioning gaze.

"I helped my mom in the kitchen since I was a little kid. I can cook for small or big groups. Though, it has been a long time since I have."

"What is your favorite thing to cook?"

Goodness, those blue eyes sent her heart fluttering.

"Comfort food. Roast chicken or beef. Potatoes, veggies. When I'm making for just for myself, I stick with salads."

"Yuck."

Madison giggled. "You have some on your plate."

"Yeah. Wanted to prove I could eat it."

Everyone laughed at Derin's joke.

As she ate the grilled chicken breast and salad, the conversation turned to Vargas Sports.

"I was thinking," Derin started. "What if we created a schedule for the athletes?"

"What would you put on it?" Cole asked.

"Stagger the schedule for Ryan and Hudson's time. Then time with all the clients for counseling or support group discussion."

Madison nodded slowly. "I like that idea. It would be nice to talk to other athletes dealing with the same fears as me."

Derin reached over and squeezed her knee under the table.

"I was thinking about Bible study for those who want to take part."

"So far, about a third of the clients who've booked are

part of the Christian Athletes Association," Cole said.

"What about time with the kids for the equine therapy program?" she offered.

Derin's eyes snapped to hers. He set his fork down and rubbed a hand over his beard. "I never thought of that."

"When I stopped by today, watching your nephew really helped me appreciate my situation isn't as dire as it feels when I obsess over it. I might not play at the same level. It might not be my source of income. But I can still enjoy playing tennis. I can find another job."

Derin nodded. "I see what you mean. Every time I stop by the arena during the equine therapy, it brightens my mood too. Those kids are amazing."

"Wouldn't it be wonderful if the athletes helped the kids as part of the equine therapy?" Syd asked.

"That's a great idea." Derin looked at Cole. "Do you think Adan would lead the Bible study? He's a former PBR champion and can relate to the athletes forced to change careers."

"I'll ask him. I like all these ideas," Cole said. "Let me draft a schedule tomorrow of different activities. Rehab. Equine therapy. Trail rides. Counseling and Bible study time. Training for their sport. Let me know if you have other ideas."

Everyone agreed as they finished the meal. Madison pushed her plate away.

"Time for one of your questions, cowboy."

Derin snorted and tossed his phone toward her. Then he stood and cleared the plates from the table. Madison opened the app and read the next question.

"What's the worst movie you've ever seen?"

Madison smiled when he answered immediately.

"That end-times movie with Nicholas Cage. Terrible. The worst *ever*."

Cole laughed. "Yeah, and why does it seem like it's on

every week on some cable channel?"

"That was pretty bad," Sydney agreed, while Madison's head bobbed up and down. "But my worst movie? *Baywatch* with The Rock. It was sooooo corny."

"Yeah, but lots of eye candy," Derin said. "For the ladies too."

Madison snorted. "I suppose. Eye candy aside, it really was a lame plot. But I think that was the intent."

"What about you, Cole?" Syd asked.

"There are plenty. What I don't get is the whole 'let's remake this mediocre movie from decades ago?' Like *Ghostbusters*. It was lame in the eighties. Why on earth did they remake it?"

"Agree," Derin said as he stuffed the last of the dirty dishes in the dishwasher. He took his seat next to Madison and asked what hers was.

"Okay, I know this isn't a movie, but I just have to say the worst ending to a TV series of all time was *Lost*. Hated it!"

Sydney and Cole agreed whole heartedly.

"I don't think I've seen it," Derin said.

Madison dropped her head to the side and quirked an eyebrow.

"We didn't watch TV. Didn't own one. So all the sports I watched growing up were at the bunkhouse. Didn't sneak out on a school night, so I missed that one."

"We should watch it," Madison offered before realizing how it might sound. "We'll just stop before the last season."

Little lines formed next to those heart-shattering blue eyes as a smile lit his face. She loved his smile.

"I'd like that."

A knock sounded from the front door, breaking the moment between them.

"Mijo! I brought dessert."

Madison's stomach knotted as Derin hurried toward the

door.

"Gracias, Mami."

When the middle-aged woman pushed past him, Madison stood. Guess she was meeting his mother tonight.

# 11

DERIN HURRIED TO greet his mother, feeling the shift in Madison's mood. He hoped Mami wouldn't make a scene. He accepted the *tres leches* cake and bag of *churros*.

"Smells good, Mami."

He tried nudging her toward the door, but failed.

"Aren't you going to introduce me to your *novia*?"

"Mami, she's not my girlfriend."

Mami raised an eyebrow and narrowed her eyes. "Si, she is."

Derin held back a growl and followed his mother over to the table. He set the desserts on the counter before he introduced Madison.

"Mami, this is Madison Moore. Madi, this is my mamacita, Catalina."

Madi smiled and offered her hand. Mami yanked Madi to her feet and pulled her in for a big hug, rocking her from side to side. Derin cringed at his mother's overly dramatic display. He wished he could see Madi's face.

"I never thought Derin would find himself a *chica*. Look at you. So *bonita*."

Madi, to her credit, took his mami's gushing in stride. She complimented her on the delicious smelling desserts.

When Mami started to sit in his chair, he held her arm and whispered through gritted teeth, "You promised."

Mami sighed in disgust with that half-pouty, half-resigned way of mamacitas. Thankfully, she allowed him to escort her to the door.

"You'll bring her for *cena familiar* soon, no?"

"Of course." Anything to get his mother to leave. She pointed to her cheek, and he pressed a kiss to it.

"Have fun, *mijo!*"

Then she whirled out the door.

Derin sighed. Guess he had better figure out how long he could put off inviting Madi to the family dinner. Knowing Mami, she would hound him several times a week until he did.

Cole dished up the desserts and had already placed them on the table by the time Derin sat in his chair again.

"So, that's your mother?" Madi winked at him.

"Yeah."

"She's delightful."

Derin groaned. "She's nosy."

"I can see where the bossy comes from." Madi's eyes glinted.

Derin snorted. "I suppose you're right."

Madi asked about the cake.

"*Tres leches* cake," he said. "Don't know exactly what it's made of, but it must use three different milks, thus *tres leches.*"

He watched as she sliced off a bite with her fork. Her lips — those plump lips — pursed over the fork. Her eyes fluttered as she chewed it, driving him mad.

"Oh, it's good. Very moist and creamy for a cake."

Derin cleared his throat, trying to clear his wayward thoughts.

"Mami's *churros* are my favorite. I enjoy dipping them in the caramel sauce she makes."

Each person spooned some caramel sauce over the fried puffy dessert coated in cinnamon and sugar.

Sydney exclaimed over the *churros*. "I've never had them before. This is delicious."

He smiled. His mami was a wonderful cook.

After they ate their fill of dessert, Madi helped him with the remaining dishes while Sydney and Cole snuggled on the couch. Yeah, he might not have a girlfriend, but Cole definitely did.

"So, I take it you haven't dated much?"

Derin froze, finger poised over the start button on the dishwasher. "Why do you ask?"

"Your mother. It sounded like you don't introduce her to many, or any, women."

He swallowed away the tightness in his throat. He and Madi might not have defined their relationship yet, but it felt like the right time to tell her about his past. Punching the start button, he turned to face her.

"Walk with me?"

"Sure."

As he led her outside, his mind churned. How could he explain his history with women without scaring her away? He liked Madi. Cared about her more than he wanted to admit. He didn't want to lose her.

They stepped onto the porch, Derin clicking the door shut behind him. The cool evening air felt good against his warm cheeks. He led Madi toward the main road to the ranch house. Maybe some day he would plant a garden and add a few walking paths in his yard.

"So..." Madi's voice trailed off.

"No. I haven't introduced my mother to any of the women I've been with."

"Been with?"

Derin cleared his throat, thankful for the veil of darkness for this difficult conversation.

"Madi, until May of last year, I..."

This sucked. Admitting the worst about himself to a

woman he respected and with whom he wanted a meaning-ful relationship. He wouldn't blame her if she ran far and fast from him.

"I haven't always... Rarely, if I'm truthful... Acted like a Christian man ought to."

"You slept around."

The disappointment in her voice hurt worse than being kicked by a bull.

"Yeah."

"How many women?"

Derin coughed, his mouth drying quickly as he did the math. One woman a week per peak season for more than a decade. That would be...

Hundreds.

The bile rose in his throat. The reality of his wretched-ness sliced through him. No woman would want him as a husband. Not Madi. No one.

"Derin?"

"Many."

"Many as in five?"

"More."

"A dozen?"

He clenched his jaw, not wanting to tell her the truth. She would leave him if he did.

"Let's just say more than a dozen."

Madi stopped walking and his heart sank.

MADISON'S HEART BROKE. She wasn't perfect either. She had slept with a few of her boyfriends. A few. Not "more than a dozen."

How many was "more than a dozen," anyway? She got the feeling it was significantly more.

"Madi, I'm sorry."

"Why? Why are you apologizing to me?" She turned to face him, hands shaking at her side. "We haven't made this—" She motioned her hand back and forth between them. "Official."

Even in the dim moonlight, Madison watched his shoulders drop.

"No chance of that now, I guess."

"That's not what I said, Derin." She exhaled loudly. "Look, I'm no saint, but I'm not like that any longer. I won't sleep with a man until marriage. If you're looking for a hookup, you're barking up the wrong tree."

"I'm not. Not anymore."

So he had been?

Madison let out a disgusted groan and turned on her heel, stumbling over the uneven ground. Derin's warm hands grasped her chilled arms, keeping her from hitting the dirt. Her hands flew to his chest—completely by accident.

When his grip loosened, she met his gaze, unable to see anything in the darkness. He reached up with one hand and cupped her cheek, sending electricity coursing down her spine.

His voice was rough when he spoke. "You are too special for something like that."

Her chest rose and fell rapidly as her pulse raced, stirred by his gentle touch. They might not have defined their relationship, but her heart didn't care. She liked the cowboy more than she wanted to admit.

"Madi."

The air heated between them. He inched his lips ever closer to hers. Seconds felt like eons. The chill she felt earlier dissipated. His breath warmed her cheek. Against her better judgement, her hands slid up his chest and hooked behind his neck, the length of his body heating hers.

What was she doing? Now wasn't the time to kiss him.

Foolish, foolish.

When his lips brushed over hers, fire coursed through her. She eagerly drank him in, despite the warning bells in her mind. She returned the kiss as if she had waited her entire life for him.

*Pull away!* Her conscience scolded her. She ignored it as his hands roamed over her back, warming every inch of her being.

Suddenly, Derin dropped his hold and took several steps away from her, swiping the back of his hand across his lips. The chill in the air froze her in place, lips stinging. She sucked in a loud breath.

"I'm sorry." He growled into the darkness. "This is exactly what I didn't want to do."

Madison wrapped her arms over her stomach as her eyes burned.

"You didn't want to kiss me?"

"Ugh! No!"

She pivoted toward his house.

"Madi, wait! That's not what I meant."

She hurried away from Derin as the tears flooded down her cheeks. Foolish, foolish woman.

"Madi!"

Strong hands clamped around her waist.

"Stop!"

When she stilled, he loosened his grip.

"Let me explain."

She didn't face him, but she stood still, waiting for him to continue.

"I've wanted to kiss you ever since we went line dancing. I think about you all the time. I want…"

Her foot tapped on the gravel drive as her ire rose.

"Just what do you want, Derin?"

"You don't understand. The distance between a kiss and sex for me is very, very short."

The air whooshed from her lungs. Confusion swirled around her. He wanted to kiss her. But he didn't. She was special, but... What? Nothing he said made sense.

"I've been in counseling. A recovery group. I have dated no one or been with anyone since last May because I don't know how to just date... Without..."

Her mind whirled. Recovery group? Counseling?

"This is more serious than just crossing a line with a girl-friend, isn't it?" she asked.

He ran both hands through his hair and tugged. Frustration rolled off him.

"I've never been in an actual relationship. Growing up with single women guests..."

Madison staggered backward as if he had punched her in the stomach. How could she have been so stupid? She gave her heart to a man who couldn't control himself — to a player. How could she ever trust him?

She couldn't live that life. Always wondering if he would be faithful.

Madison started to shake. How could Derin lead her on like that?

"It's over," she tossed over her shoulder as she jogged toward his house.

"Madi! I'm not like that anymore. Please, give me a chance!"

She bolted up the porch stairs and flung the door open.

"Take me home," she demanded from Cole.

"Madison, what's wrong?" Syd asked.

"Just take me home." She bit the inside of her cheek to stem the flood.

"Alright. I will," Cole said.

She exited Derin's house, rage and heartache powering her tears. When Cole disarmed his car, she yanked the door open. Syd squished onto the passenger seat with her. Stupid two-seater car. It had been funny on the way over. Now,

Madison just wanted away from Derin. Away from everyone.

Cole turned on the car and drove away. They passed Derin. When the headlights flashed over his face, Madison noticed the despair in his eyes which fractured her resolve.

It didn't matter. He lied to her, and she could never trust him again.

The moment Cole parked his car in front of the casita, Madison shoved the car door open and darted toward the looming wood door, digging her key card from her purse. She yanked it open and stormed to her room, flopping face down on her bed. The sobs shook her body.

What was wrong with her—always falling for the wrong men? Her last boyfriend, Evan, had only been out to further his career by association. Derin just wanted a hookup.

A pinch in her gut vied for attention. If Derin had truly been looking for a one-night stand, he had plenty of opportunities with her. The night after line dancing. After the horse ride. After dinner in town two weeks ago.

*Lord, I don't know what to believe — what to think.*

"Madison?" Syd's voice came from the doorway. "You wanna talk?"

"No." Her voice creaked, and she sniffled. "Sorry to ruin your night. Go. Spend time with Cole."

"You sure?"

"Yeah."

The soft click of the door latching floated across the room. Alone again.

Madison's tears came stronger as the heartache hit her anew. She really cared for Derin. He seemed so genuine. Those one hundred and one questions... Who did that if they just wanted something physical?

No one.

The words felt like they echoed in the room, even though she hadn't said them aloud. Madison sat up and wiped the tears from her cheeks. Maybe she had judged him too harshly.

Exhaustion washed over her. The stress of her injury, the surgery, the rehab—all seemed to pile on top of her. She stood and washed her face in the en suite. Then she changed into pjs and went to bed, leaving all the mess in her heart for another day.

# 12

DERIN STOOD ROOTED to the ground like a giant Pondero-sa pine. His stomach threatened to toss Mami's *churros* at his feet. With each step Madi took away from him, he felt her rejection ripping him in two.

Nothing about that conversation went well. He had been unprepared. Rushed it. Said too much and not enough all at the same time.

Fisting hands at his side, he strolled back toward his temporary home. He should have waited to talk to his recovery group. Gotten ideas on how to have the ugly conversation before stumbling through it and torching his relationship with Madi.

Ugh!

Derin had never loved a woman. Never thought about how many he had been with. Several hundred. Impossible for him to remember most of their names. His stomach churned again.

He didn't blame Madi for her disgust. It was how he felt about himself.

Did his family know the extent of his problem? He had been blind for so long. Chalked it up to male hormones. Sewing his wild oats. A phase he would grow out of.

Except he never did. The only reason he stopped was because of Nicole.

The lights from Cole's McLaren flashed over him, blinding him from seeing the inside of the car. He had lost Madi. Maybe forever. All because he couldn't control himself. Didn't get help sooner.

It had taken a situation like Nicole to jolt him from his stupidity.

Every time he hooked up with a woman, it was completely consensual. If there was even a hint the woman wasn't interested, he walked away. They had all been single, too.

Even Janessa — Dalton's ex-fiancée — that relationship lasted only until Derin discovered she had been dating both Dalton and him at the same time. The moment he found out, he broke things off. Said nothing to Dalton and never touched her again. There were just some lines he refused to cross.

Until Nicole.

She came to the resort alone. No ring on her finger. Flirted with him, coming on very strong. So, of course, he pursued something with her. A few nights of wild passion. In hind sight, it hadn't been worth it.

Their third night together in her room — it was always in the guest's room — he had been caught up. Missed noticing a second suitcase. She had initiated intimacy with him, and he gladly obliged.

Then her husband walked in on them. Nicole never mentioned a spouse. Never acted like she was in any kind of relationship. Derin didn't know until her husband's fist cracked against his jaw.

Derin grabbed his clothes and hurried from the room, ducking into the closest supply closet at the end of the hall.

That's when he realized he was out of control. He couldn't keep living like that.

Cole was the only person he told. Despite his shock, Cole suggested Derin go to counseling with a Christian counselor. That advice turned out to be the best he had ever received.

His counselor helped Derin work through why he did what he did. How it was more than just sewing wild oats. That he was trying to fill up some brokenness deep in his heart. Jealousy toward Drake and even Devon, to some extent. He loved his little brothers and didn't understand why he coveted the attention Mami lavished on the youngest two. But when the counselor uncovered that secret, it rang true to Derin.

The counselor gave him tools to learn self-control that would help him stop using intimacy to fill the emptiness in his soul. He recommended the recovery group. The group was a lifeline. Derin learned he wasn't alone in his struggles. He also learned it was possible to change and live a godly life by watching their example.

The more time he spent in his recovery group, Derin hoped he could change. He began dreaming about a wife, a family of his own.

And when he met Madison, he foolishly believed that he had found a woman he could date who might like him, sins and all.

How very wrong he was. The pain of rejection seared through him, hotter than an old-fashioned branding iron.

Derin eased the door of his house open. The TV blared a movie. The emotional music of a chick flick echoed throughout the great room. After confirming he was alone, he punched the power button on the remote. In the silence, Derin thought he could hear his heart breaking.

He collapsed onto the couch and texted his group. He asked for a prayer for him and Madi after telling them he botched explaining his past.

*Lord, I know I don't deserve Madi. I know I've been an idiot. Help me stay strong. I want Your Will in this relationship even if it's different from mine. I don't want to live like I have been for the last decade of my life. You promised to make me new. Show me how, even in my brokenheartedness. Be with Madi. Surround her with Your love. Help her find a man who will love her more than life itself.*

The last remnant of his heart melted within his chest and pooled at his feet. Whoever thought living a surrendered life was easy had to be a fool. This was the hardest thing he had ever done. Harder than wrestling a steer to the ground or staying on the back of a bucking bronco. Harder than leading a group of rough-edged men.

Maybe God would grant him peace in time. How long it would take, he did not know.

ON WEDNESDAY MORNING, Madison considered avoiding the gym. With the big charity tournament next week, she couldn't skip a workout. Yet the thought of accidentally running into Derin made her stomach turn. She had successfully avoided him since last Friday and didn't think her luck would hold out much longer.

She donned her workout clothes and strolled toward the sports complex. Derin's truck sat in its usual spot, right next to Cole's lime green sports car.

Memories from last Friday crashed over her. Derin's stirring kiss which caused her to lose hours of sleep every night. His confession. Her fear and doubt.

Madison bit her lower lip to keep the emotion stuffed deep down. She must focus on her job, not the man who turned her heart upside down.

She yanked the door of the complex open, nearly colliding with the broad-shouldered man she was trying to forget. His warm hands wrapped lightly around her upper arms to steady her, then released her promptly as if she had burned him.

"Sorry," he said as he stepped to the side.

She forced a cheery tone. "No worries."

Then she darted around him, half-jogging toward the gym. The compulsion to look over her shoulder was strong, but she ignored it.

Madison popped in her earbuds and headed straight for the treadmill. She pushed her body hard, allowing the strain of her muscles to hide the pain in her heart. By the time she finished her cardio workout, the rush of endorphins barely hid her heartache.

She met Bella Gaines at the tennis court, like most mornings. Her practice went fine, though she suspected Bella held back. Probably at Layla's request to give Madison's shoulder time to heal.

By the time she showered back at the casita, she had slipped into a full-blown melancholy. She punched the contact in her phone for her mom. It rang a few times before she picked up.

"Madison!"

"Hi, Mom."

"It's so good to hear your voice. You up for a video call?"

Madison sighed. "I guess."

They switched over and as soon as her mom's face came into view, Madison's eyes burned.

"What's wrong, honey?"

"I broke things off with Derin."

"Why? It sounded like you really liked him. And that he's a Christian."

"He's a player, Mom."

"Really? It didn't sound like it from what you've said before."

Madison shared the highlights of her conversation last Friday with her mom.

"So, what makes you think he's a player now? It sounds like he's been working very hard to change."

Madison looked away. He had said he had not been with anyone since last May. And he talked about counseling and a recovery group.

"Hmm. I see you're thinking about it. May I make a suggestion?"

"Always, Mom."

"Read John 8. See if that gives you some perspective."

Madison caught up on the news from the ranch. Nothing earth shattering. Her older brother, Mason, started dating one of the Yardley girls. She knew the younger one from high school. Not the best home life, but maybe they turned out fine.

When she finished the call, she changed into jeans, boots, and a loose blouse before heading over to the stables. Adan Franco greeted her as she scuffed down the alleyway.

"Madison, what brings you by?"

"I thought a horse ride might do me some good."

He asked about her experience with horses and she told him she grew up riding on her family's ranch.

"You want some company? I've got two horses that could use some exercise. One is perfect for you."

"Sure."

"This is Frappe."

Madison snorted. "We've met."

"Perfect. Would you mind grooming her?"

When Adan handed her the bridle and lead, she took it and led the dappled gray to the grooming area. He brought a palomino for himself. Then he grabbed two saddles from the tack room and placed them nearby.

Madison picked Frappe's hooves before retrieving the currycomb. She ran the comb over the horse's back and sides. Then she used a brush in short flicking motions over the mare's body.

The routine actions brought a wave of nostalgia. She missed the view of the snow-capped Rockies to the east of her family's ranch. Cold winter nights around the fireplace. Early mornings to feed and care for the animals.

Her life had been in the spotlight for so long, she had forgotten life on the ranch. Though the scenery surrounding Vargas Ranch looked very different, it reminded her of how simple her early years had been. She missed the slower pace.

She cleaned Frappe's face with a soft sponge. Then she placed the blanket and saddle on the horse. After cinching the strap, she led her outside. Madison mounted the mare and waited for Adan.

"How long would you like to ride?" he asked.

"Not much more than an hour. I'm still out of practice."

Lines crinkled beside his eyes with his laughter.

"I'll go easy on ya."

She followed behind Adan until they left the resort property. He took her on a different trail from the one she rode with Derin, Cole, and Syd. This one headed east, then south.

Beautiful green grass covered the desert floor, dotted by tiny bright yellow flowers. Tall saguaro cacti reached toward the deep blue sky. Green covered the spikey spindles of the ocotillo cacti and red flowers sat primly on top of them. The crisp air renewed her spirit.

"What's on your mind?" Adan's voice cut through the stillness.

Madison let out a very long breath. "What's not on mind? I think that would be a shorter list."

"You worried about your career?"

"Yeah. That and…"

"Derin?"

She twisted in her saddle to look at him.

"Noticed you two avoiding each other."

"Yeah. We had a falling out. My mom thinks I need to

read John 8."

"Hmm." Adan pulled out his phone and tapped a few times. "Ah, yes. That's the story about Jesus writing in the dirt."

"Oh, I know that one. The religious leaders caught a woman in adultery and brought her to Jesus."

"They expected him to agree to stone her. Instead, he crouched down and started writing in the dirt. Then he told them whoever was without sin should cast the first stone. He continued writing. Then, one by one, the religious leaders walked away."

Madison's stomach roiled. She had judged Derin too harshly.

"Then," Adan continued, "Jesus told her he wouldn't condemn her. He told her to go and sin no more."

She looked over the flat pasture land. *Lord, forgive me. I didn't listen, and I condemned Derin.*

"Have you noticed a change in Derin?" she asked.

"Since you broke up?"

Heat warmed her cheeks. "I mean from last year."

"Yeah. He's a different man. Comes to Bible study without fail. Attends church and takes notes now. Doesn't hang around the resort in the evenings."

Madison nodded. She had been wrong. Very wrong about him.

"Did you know he asked Cole to move here? Asked him to be an accountability partner. And Cole came to take the job at a significantly lower salary from what he made as an agent."

"Cole has always been a stand-up guy."

"And he believes in Derin. So do I. So do his brothers."

"Guess I owe him an apology."

Adan said nothing for several minutes. Then he mentioned he used to be a world champion bull rider.

"Really? Why did you quit?"

A shadow moved over his features. "It's a long story. Let's just say that God made it clear it was time for me to leave. I tried to avoid it for a while, believing I could win the championship for a fourth year in a row. He got my attention in a way I couldn't dodge. So, I came back here and Dylan gave me a job. Now I'm close to my family working at a job I love. I get to be involved in my nephew's life. Started a charity for him and others like him."

Madison sniffed. "I keep hoping that my career isn't over. Yet I can't shake the feeling that it is."

"So, what's your next step?"

She shook her head. "I don't know."

"I'll pray for you, Madison. That God will make your path clear."

"Thanks."

Silence settled for several minutes before Adan spoke again.

"If you don't mind, I'll leave you with your thoughts. Just turn around on this trail when you're ready. It'll take you straight to the stables."

"Thanks for everything."

Adan touched his fingertips to the edge of his hat. Then he kicked his horse into a trot before pushing her to a canter. A cloud of dust hid his form from view.

Madison might not have clarity about her career, but she knew what she needed to do in her relationship. Hopefully, Derin would forgive her and they could move past her stupidity.

# 13

THURSDAY EVENING, DERIN drove toward Wickenburg, lower than he had been in a long time. He even texted Jeff to watch for him, just so he wouldn't chicken out of going to his recovery group meeting. When he parked in the church parking lot, Jeff stepped out of the shadows.

"Glad you made it."

"Thanks for…"

He matched Jeff's shorter strides as they entered the building. Once inside the meeting room, Jeff spoke again.

"Rough week?"

"Yeah. Like I texted, she broke up with me."

"What did you say to her?"

Derin told the guys about their conversation, leaving out his poorly timed kiss.

"I don't think any woman is going to want to settle down with someone like me."

Pete, the one hundred and one questions guy, snorted. "If I can convince a wonderful Christian woman to marry me, you can, too."

"What's that supposed to mean?"

Ian laughed. "He means your good looks and the fact that you're a cowboy puts you at the top of most women's wish lists."

Derin rolled his eyes.

The leader, Anderson, jumped in. "The right woman will not hold your past against you. Keep leaning on God, bro. Let Him guide you and let the future worry about itself."

Derin folded his arms over his chest and frowned. He wanted Madi. Not some future woman he had yet to meet. Madi was the woman for him. He knew it soul deep.

Yet the sting of her rejection felt as strong as nearly a week ago. He wished he could turn back time and make better choices. He wished he would have realized sooner what a mess he was.

None of that mattered. He could not change the past. Anderson was right. He needed to focus on his relationship with God and let the future unfold however it did.

Derin thought he had been doing a good job of that right up to Friday afternoon when Madi knocked on his office door.

His stomach clenched as he took in her appearance. She leaned against the doorframe, dressed in a bright pink dress that flared at her narrow waist. The cap sleeves showed off her sculpted arms. Berry-colored lip gloss covered her plump lips. Her long lashes fanned over her tanned cheeks as she looked down. When her eyes finally met his, his breath hitched.

"Can I come in?"

Derin nodded, unable to speak. Hurt and anger rushed forward before he squelched them. He would hear her out. He cared about her too much not to.

Madi tucked the flowy skirt close to her leg with one sweeping motion as she eased into the chair across from him. Then she rested her hands in her lap.

"I owe you an apology."

The words bounced off his chest before they registered fully in his mind. His heart raced. Dare he hope?

"It was wrong of me to hold your past against you. I'm

sorry."

Her apology settled over the broken cracks in his heart. Maybe he still had a chance with Madi.

"The Derin I've come to know over the past two months is nothing like the man you told me about. You are considerate. Funny. Confident." She shrugged. "Maybe a little bossy, at times."

A smile tilted one side of his mouth.

"And from what I've observed, your heart belongs to God."

The thin smile faded from his mouth as he struggled to receive the words that proved he had changed. Derin's throat worked and his breath quickened.

"He doesn't condemn you, so who am I to?"

The thickness in his throat made it hard to speak. "Madi."

"I'm sorry, Derin. I had no right to judge you or to assume you couldn't overcome your past—especially since you are leaning on God. The counseling and recovery group prove your desire to live forgiven as a new creation."

Madi's lovely brown eyes flitted to the floor. She rubbed her hands on the arms of the chair before she pushed to her feet.

"Anyway. I hope you can forgive me."

In two swift strides, he drew her into his arms. When her arms wrapped around his middle, he guided her head against his chest, the warmth of her body filled his heart to overflowing. Of course, he forgave her. He loved her.

Love. A foreign emotion to him seeped through his heart. Yeah. He loved Madison Moore.

"I forgive you," he whispered into her hair, with a rough edge to his tone.

He felt Madi sag against him, squeezing him tight. Derin didn't want to release her. He could stay like that all night. Just holding her close to his heart. Each breath and heartbeat were in sync with hers.

Several minutes passed before Madi leaned back. A half-smile quirked the side of her mouth.

"Can I take you to dinner?"

He smiled and shrugged. "I could eat."

Her hands slid down his arms and squeezed his hands before she released him.

"Um. Would you mind driving? I don't know your favorite restaurant and I don't have a car."

A deep chuckle erupted from his mouth. "So, you're asking me out?"

"Yeah."

He tossed his keys to her. "You drive."

She caught them mid-air. "Oh, no, cowboy. Your truck intimidates me."

Derin clasped her hand and led her outside. Then he held the driver's side door open for her. He pressed the seat button to scoot it closer to the steering wheel before stepping aside and offering her his hand.

"You're serious, aren't you?" Madi's eyes widened.

"You're a country gal. It's just a truck."

"Fine."

She gathered her skirt and climbed behind the wheel. He stifled another laugh when she moved the seat even closer. Then he jogged around to the other side and eased into the passenger seat.

"I could get used to you wooing me."

Madi laughed. "Is that what I'm doing?"

"You know it is."

Derin looked up one question from the app before he punched in the info for his favorite restaurant. When the truck turned over, Madi backed out like a pro and followed the navigation instructions.

After she pulled onto the main highway, he asked, "What do you like but are afraid to admit?"

MADISON BLEW OUT a soft breath. Just like that, she and Derin were back on steady ground. He forgave her and moved on in the same instant. Unbelievable. She had been foolish for thinking he could not change.

"Can you repeat the question?"

"What do you like but are afraid to admit?"

*You.* No way she would say that aloud.

Instead, she protested. "Ugh. Is it me, or are these questions getting harder?"

"Stop dodging, Madi."

"Fine. I kinda like driving this truck."

"No dice, princess."

"Yeah. You're still bossy."

"Some things won't change."

A smile spread across her lips. She hoped not. She liked his directness.

"Snuggling in front of a fireplace with a handsome boyfriend."

"I don't think I should let that one count."

"Is there a rulebook for these questions?"

Derin chuckled, and the sound warmed her heart. She liked their banter. The tension from earlier unwound from her shoulders.

"I think the intent is something like 'I like Brussels sprouts.'"

"You do?"

"As a matter of fact, I enjoy roasted sprouts with bacon."

Madison scoffed. "And when have you eaten them?"

"Chef makes them when they are in season. And the steakhouse we're going to serves them as a side dish."

"This I have to see."

"Are you prejudiced against Brussels sprouts?"

Madison laughed, and the dregs of her earlier anxiety disappeared completely.

"I think I'd have to try some of yours to see if they are any good."

"Get ready to be wowed."

The navigation instructed her to turn off the freeway. She listened carefully for the rest of the directions. At last, they arrived, and she parked in a space with no one on either side.

"Chicken."

Madison knew he meant her parking. She quipped, "At a steakhouse? I think not."

"Stay put."

Derin hopped out of the truck and rounded the back before opening the door for her.

"Wait, I thought I was supposed to be wooing you."

After he closed the door, he leaned close and nipped at her ear. "Later."

Heat warmed her cheeks and sent waves of warmth rolling over her. Thankfully, the crisp evening air cooled them quickly.

"You look amazing, by the way. It's like you knew I would have to forgive you, dressing up like that."

"Stop it." Madison giggled and lightly swatted his arm.

Derin put in their name with the hostess, then took a seat next to her in the waiting area.

"Twenty minutes. Time for another question."

He opened the app and handed it to her. "You read it."

Madison smiled as her fingers brushed against his. She loved the questions and she might just love this man.

"What's the strangest way you've ever made a friend?"

Derin chuckled. "Cole."

"Oh? How did you meet?"

"He came to the resort and wanted the full guest ranch

experience. Horse riding. Roping lessons. Back then, we even did old-fashioned branding demos."

"I hated leading those activities. It felt cheap to me. So my brothers devised a plan to make sure I had to lead at least one out of three times. This was back when it was just me, Dalton, and Dylan working on the ranch. Dev and Drake were still in high school."

"How did they make sure you led your fair share?" she asked, angling toward him. His eyes glinted.

"Straws. We drew straws, and I drew the short one. What I didn't know until later is that they made me draw first and all the straws were the same length."

"Sneaky. I'll bet that was Dalton's idea."

"Padre's. He's my grandfather. The old coot has a trick or two up his sleeve."

Madison giggled. Then she laced her fingers with his as his hand rested on his knee. Being there with him felt like home. She pushed the disturbing thought aside.

"Anyway, I ended up on a three-day, two-night camping excursion with Cole. It turned out to be the best time. Even though we came from completely different worlds, he quickly earned my respect. He gave every task two hundred percent. Never shied away from the difficult."

Derin's gaze dropped to their hands, and she held her breath, waiting for him to continue.

"Through it all, he talked about God like He was his best friend. I went to church—couldn't grow up a Vargas and not. But everything about Cole seemed authentic. I asked him questions and learned from him. We became firm friends. Kept in touch long after he left."

"Wow. I did not know how deep your friendship ran."

"I'm glad he's here now. I couldn't run Vargas Sports without him."

"Derin, party of two?" the hostess asked.

"That's us."

Derin stood and allowed Madison to follow behind the hostess as she led them to a table. After they ordered, Derin asked Madison the same question.

"The strangest way I met a friend... Has to be Bella Gaines."

"Your tennis friend?"

"Yeah. We met at the Olympic trials. She's from Arizona. I was from Colorado. She's a city girl. I was a country girl—odd for the sport of tennis."

Derin winked at her. "Not too odd."

Heat warmed her cheeks. She sipped her ice water before continuing.

"We hit it off instantly. We warmed up together and practiced together. She told me about her crazy family. I shared about life on the ranch. After I qualified and she didn't, she told me she would pray for me. We exchanged numbers and have kept in touch ever since."

"Sounds like a good friend."

Madison smiled before frowning. "Yeah, she's really been there for me since the US Open."

When Derin reached across the table for her hand, she looked up and met his gaze. His thumb rubbed over the back of her hand.

"I'm praying for you too, Madi."

"Thanks. It means a lot."

When the server set their meals on the table, Derin took her hand and prayed over it. Then a grin spread across his handsome, bearded face.

"Time to try something new, Madi."

He speared a roasted Brussels sprout with bacon bits and held his fork out to her. Madison felt her cheeks heat.

"Maybe you should try it first," she suggested.

"Not a chance. Come on. You're braver than that."

She sighed loudly and leaned forward, letting her lips pull the scary green vegetable from his fork. When she bit into it, an explosion of flavor danced on her tongue. Tangy. Salty. Crispy, charred goodness.

Madison's eyes rounded as she swallowed the bite. "That was so good."

Derin winked at her. "Would I ever lead you astray?"

She ignored his comment. "I know the bacon provides some of the saltiness. What makes it tangy?"

"I figure it's the balsamic vinegar."

"I have to learn how to make this. It's so good."

As Derin sliced off a piece of his steak, he cleared his throat. Madison paused, chewing her own bite slowly as his gaze grew intense.

"Would you... On Sunday, would you come to our family dinner with me?"

She swallowed the bite in her mouth, nearly choking. After she recovered from a brief coughing fit, she took a deep breath.

"You want me to meet your family?"

When he ducked his head, his sudden bashfulness surprised her. He cleared his throat before meeting her gaze.

"Yes." His head nodded. "Yes, I would like you to meet my family."

"Then, of course, I'll come."

Derin grinned, his smile as radiant as the sun. It warmed Madison all the way to her toes. Guess she was going to meet the entire Vargas clan.

# 14

---

SUNDAY MORNING DAWNED and Derin tried to shake off his nerves. Not only was Madi coming to Sunday supper, but she planned to attend cowboy church. Sit next to him. It felt extremely significant to him.

It might be a mistake. She could run away again. It took a strong woman to accept his past. But Madi was strong. Stronger than she realized.

Derin rubbed a hand over his face as he stared into the mirror. He might be a handsome man on the outside, but he felt disfigured and gruesome on the inside. Some days, he couldn't believe God had changed him. He doubted if it would last. And he didn't blame Madi for doubting it, too.

He snagged his phone and thumbed out a message to his group. *Need prayer. Madi coming to church with me. Meeting my family. Tearing me up inside.*

Jeff's response came swiftly. *Praying.*

Pete answered quickly, too. *Therefore, if anyone is in Christ, he is a new creation. The old has passed away; behold, the new has come.*

2 Corinthians 5:17. Derin closed his eyes, bracing his palms against the bathroom countertop. He repeated the verse in his mind again and again. *Lord, Jesus, I want to be in You. I want to believe what You say is true. That the old me has passed away and I am a new creation. Help my unbelief!*

An image formed in his mind. Madison Moore walking down the aisle toward him in a white dress. Brown eyes alive with joy as she took his hand. Derin faced her, pledging his whole heart and soul to her. Her smile grew, and she wrapped him in her arms. His family beamed.

Derin's eyes flew open. It couldn't be possible, could it?

He shook off his doubt and spritzed on some cologne. He had trimmed the wildness from his beard yesterday. Then he grabbed his black cowboy hat with a fancy silver band—his church hat. Running a hand down the buttons of the bright blue shirt, he smiled, pleased with his appearance.

Cole waited for him in the living room.

"Coffee?"

"Sure."

Cole poured him a travel mug full of the fresh brew before they took off in his truck to pick up Madi and Sydney. He drank a large gulp of the scalding coffee. Then he killed the engine.

Madi stepped from the shade of the patio. Her gauzy white dress rippled in the breeze. The modest neckline and three-quarters sleeves enhanced her country-style appeal. Her brown cowgirl boots sent his heart racing. She wore a long gold chain with a delicate horse figurine that looked like it ran straight toward him.

Derin struggled to maintain control of potent emotions as he took in her appearance. Emotions—not lust. Not an attraction. Something wholesome that spoke to the deepest recesses of his heart.

*Thank you, Lord. For Madi. For this perplexing change, You've born in me. Let me learn to look at her with love. Let me cherish her.*

He tugged his hat a little lower as he swallowed down the foreign feelings, blinking away the sting in his eyes. After one last cough to mask his lack of control, he exited the truck.

Cole escorted Sydney to the back seat of Derin's extended cab dually before sliding in next to her.

Derin took Madi's hand.

"You look lovely." His voice came out scratchy.

She reached for his hat and eased it up slightly.

"Not bad, cowboy. Look at you, matching your clothes."

She winked at him. Derin smiled, appreciating her humor, which softened the intensity of the moment.

Once Madi sat securely in the passenger side, he slid behind the wheel and drove them to church.

"What is your hometown church like?" he asked.

Madi blew out a loud breath. "We sang a lot of traditional hymns. On special occasions, we sang one or two contemporary songs. Mom said our pastor finally retired two years ago."

"Wow," Cole said. "He's the only pastor you remember growing up?"

"Yeah. What about you?"

"Seemed like a new pastor started every five to seven years at my home church in California."

"Was it a big church?" Sydney asked.

"Mega church, yeah. It grew from three thousand people to nearly ten thousand before I left for college."

Derin snorted. He hadn't realized Cole came from such a large church. "Ours must feel small to you."

"I like it. We sing songs I know, and the pastor teaches strong Biblically based messages. It's not so large you can't get to know people."

"Five hundred seems large to me," Derin said. "I remember when it was about one hundred and fifty people."

"It's grown that much?" Sydney asked.

"More people are moving to Wickenburg, so the population has grown in the last five years. A few other ranches have expanded into tourism too. Many of the new residents like the feel of a cowboy church."

"Huh," Madi said. "Syd, did you grow up in church?"

"No. I only became a Christian right before I started working for you."

"Really? I didn't know that."

"Yeah. With our travel schedules, I've never been able to settle into a consistent church."

Derin glanced over at Madi, noticing her slight frown. He reached over and squeezed her hand for a few seconds before pulling into a parking space at church.

They arrived early enough for him to introduce her to most of his family. Padre had stayed home, preferring to watch online given his frequent pain. His sister-in-law, River, taught Padre how to watch from her laptop.

During the service, Derin snuck a few peeks at Madi. She worshipped with abandon, took notes on her phone from the sermon, and seemed fully engaged.

MADISON LOOPED HER hand in the crook of Derin's arm as he escorted her into the massive ranch house. She kept her jaw from gaping, barely. It had to be twice as large as her parents' home, and she had thought it was big.

The beautiful floor to ceiling windows in the enormous great room allowed sunlight to filter in. The southwestern decor felt cozy to her, reminding her of the decor in the dining hall. She released his arm and spun in a circle, taking it all in.

"It's beautiful."

Derin offered a lopsided grin that sent her heart skittering.

"I'm considering hiring the same interior designer for my house. Just need to complete the plans with the architect and build it first."

"Will it be as large as this?"

"Probably not. My grandparents built this to support two generations of adults under one roof, giving each couple privacy. I don't need something with separate wings."

After he gave her the tour, Madison insisted on helping in the kitchen. Dalton entered from the back door with a huge tray of pork shoulders.

"Just in time, Madison," Catalina said. "Here's an apron. Maybe Derin can help you tie it, no?"

Madison's cheeks warmed as she slipped the plain black apron over her head. When she reached behind her back, Derin took the strings from her, whispering in her ear, the heat of his breath warming her skin.

"I've got it."

After he loosely tied it, his hands lingered on her waist. The heat of his body behind her sent thrilling waves of electricity through her.

"Need me to show you how to pull the pork?"

His arms came around each side of her as Dalton set one tray in front of her. Derin picked up a pair of claw-looking things. Then he braced one against the hunk of meat, using the other to scrape thin strands of pork from it.

"I… Think I've got it."

Madison took the utensils. Derin placed his large hands over hers and helped for another minute.

"Mijo, you're making your *novia* blush."

Derin placed a kiss on her cheek and stepped back.

Dalton grinned at his wife, River. "Need help?"

"I've got this, cowboy."

"Drat. Upstaged by my little brother."

River laughed. "Don't you need to bring in the chicken from the smoker?"

"Fine." Dalton huffed.

"Ay!" Catalina shrieked as her husband came up behind her. He spun her around and planted a big kiss on her lips.

"Don't want my bonita, Lina, thinking her sons can out-do her husband."

"Tres!" Catalina's face reddened, and she playfully swatted at her husband.

Madison smiled at their antics while Catalina shooed all the men out of the kitchen.

"Brisa, Renata, can you prepare the cilantro lime relish? Solana, Heidi, salsa?"

Madison continued working the pork into small strands as the kitchen became a flurry of activity. Catalina and Katie, Derin's aunt, pressed and heated homemade tortillas in a cast-iron skillet.

"Smells amazing in here," Madison said.

"Family dinners are wonderful," River said. "I love the camaraderie in the kitchen. And Dalton has really become a pro at using the smoker."

"Under Padre's close supervision," Renata said.

"Of course."

"Do you have Mexican food a lot?" Madison asked.

"Fairly often. Dalton and Catalina figured pork carnitas and pulled chicken tacos would be an easy meal for the size-able crowd. We made several desserts yesterday."

"I can hardly wait to taste everything."

"Most family meals are just Dalton's brothers and their families, along with Catalina, Tres, and Padre. Today, Brisa, Dylan's wife, invited her parents and brother. Then we have you, Cole, Sydney. And Tres' brother, Diego. His wife, Katie, and their daughters Renata and Solana, who I think you've met at the resort, right?"

"Yeah. Everyone is so welcoming."

"Glad to hear it," River said.

"Do you work at the resort, too?" Madison asked as they finished the pulled pork.

River grabbed both trays and placed them in the warming oven.

"No. I'm a romance author. Most recently, I write contemporary Christian cowboy romances."

Madison giggled. "I'm sure the ranch provides plenty of inspiration."

"It does."

"Mami." Derin entered the kitchen again. "Should we set the tables?"

"Si. And find out what everyone wants to drink. We have lemonade, tea, and soda."

Derin winked at Madi. "Soda is the code word for Coke. You can always tell when it's a special family dinner. Mami breaks out the good stuff."

"Ay! Mijo. And don't you forget it. It's not every day we get to eat with someone famous."

"Hey!" River exclaimed.

Catalina laughed. "Oh, I guess we do."

Madison smiled at the family banter. She grabbed some silverware and helped Derin set the table—er, tables. A smaller table sat next to the large dining table. Only a few chairs sat around it.

"Don't worry. We won't put you at the troublemaker's table," Derin teased.

"But you'll be there, right?"

"Naw. I'm on my best behavior today."

"Doubt that," Drake said, nudging his older brother. "Madison, what would you like to drink?"

She asked for iced tea right before the room filled with people carrying serving dishes full of aromatic food. Her stomach growled as Derin held out a chair for her. Then he sat next to her.

Before Madison knew it, heads bowed and Tres offered a beautiful blessing over the food. Then every voice in the room lifted.

"We do not deviate from Your plan. Amen."

The hair on Madison's arms stood on end. "That's on the

menus in the dining hall."

"Si, Madison," Catalina said. "It is our *familia* motto."

"My mother," Padre said, voice gravelly, "wrote it shortly after we started the place back in 1952."

"Wow. And you all recite it at every meal?"

"Every family meal," Derin said. "And with the cowboys. Whenever several of us gather."

"It reminds us we serve the Lord. Everything we have is His to do with as He pleases," Tres said.

Madison let the words stir in her soul. The charity tournament would start tomorrow. Her future could shift. Yet, her skills as a tennis player were in God's hands. She wanted to follow His plan, no matter what. She just wasn't certain what it was. Perhaps He would make it clear soon.

"W-w-we have some exciting news," Dylan announced. He visibly swallowed and his wife smiled, resting a hand on his leg.

"I am officially Braden's dad."

Madison watched as Brisa's eyes reddened. Braden cheered. Soon, the family offered their congratulations to the family. Her own eyes stung, even though they were strangers to her.

She angled toward Derin. "Congratulations. I guess that makes you an official uncle now."

He squeezed her hand for a few seconds. The shimmer in his eyes told her how he viewed the news.

Derin leaned forward. "Congrats, Dyl, Brisa, and Braden. We're happy for you."

Madison couldn't help wondering what it might be like to be Braden's aunt—becoming part of this family. The thought shocked her to the core. She brushed it away quickly, before working on her meal in silence.

By the end of the meal, her worries faded away, and she enjoyed getting to know the Vargas family more.

# 15

---

"MIJO, SHE'S PERFECT."

"Mami," Derin said, warning his mother as he carried stacks of dishes into the kitchen.

His mother wiped her hands on her apron before she placed a hand on his bearded face. Her golden eyes studied his for a long moment. The smoky aroma of the carnitas still lingered in the kitchen.

"Si, you love her."

It wasn't a question. How Mami could read him so well, he did not know. It scared him a little.

"What will you do when she leaves?"

Derin set the dishes on the counter with a soft clank. Then clasped his mother's hand in his as he looked away before releasing it. "I don't know."

"Will you follow her?"

Following her from city to city with no job of his own—the idea knotted his stomach. Too much time to slip into old behavior. He would be miserable.

"I don't think I can. I'm needed here. Besides, what would I do traveling with her as she plays tennis?"

"What if she retires?"

His shoulders sagged as he exhaled. "Is it too soon to ask her to stay? She would be perfect to lead several programs—a woman's Bible study, equine therapy. Did you know she grew up on a ranch?"

Mami smiled. "I can see why she's captured your heart, mijo."

Derin ran a hand through his hair before he stuffed the dirty dishes into the dishwasher. The silverware tinked as he dropped each piece into the holder. Of course, Mami saw everything clearly. Sometimes more clearly than he saw things himself.

"I will pray for you, mijo. That God would show you both His plan for you."

"Gracias, Mami."

"Now, go take her for a walk in the garden, no?"

"Si, Mami."

Derin started the dishwasher. Then he found Madi on the back porch, under the shade of an umbrella, chatting with River. The two seemed engrossed in conversation, so he hung back, content to watch them. The faint smell of the smoker faded as a breeze blew across the patio.

"Come sit," Padre said, voice scratchy as he patted a chair next to him in the porch's shade.

Derin sat as a coughing fit shook his grandfather's frail frame. Derin leaned forward, ready to lend aid, but Padre raised his hand, warning him off.

"I'm fine." Padre sipped a glass of water. "Your girl-friend is really sweet."

"Thanks."

A few seconds passed as Derin worked up the courage to ask his grandfather something that had been on his mind.

"How did you know Grandma Elena was right for you?"

Padre chuckled before it turned into a coughing spell again. At length, he finally answered. "I knew the moment I met her."

"Oh." Not helpful.

"But that kind of love is rare. Sometimes a man knows

quickly, but it takes his woman more time to figure it out. Like Dylan. He loved Brisa for years before she grew to love him. Other times, she knows right away, like your mamacita. She knew Tres was the man for her. Took him the better part of two years before he figured it out."

Derin frowned. He had only known Madi for two months. Yet he cared for her deeply. He thought about her all the time. And he wanted to ease her burden. Certainly, it had to be love. Would she need more time to know?

He ran a hand over his beard. She had run away from him once. What if he slipped up? Would she reject him again?

"What if I hurt her?"

Padre slapped a hand on his leg as his guffaw drew the attention of a few others. As he wiped away tears from the corner of his eyes, he said, "Silly boy. Of course you'll hurt her."

His heart lurched at his grandfather's lack of confidence in him. "I don't want to."

"'Course not. But you will. Do you think in thirty-something years of marriage, your papi never hurt your mami? And she never hurt him?"

Derin shook his head.

"No one means to hurt the ones they love, but we all do. Not just our spouse."

Derin stared down at his hands. "What if I cheat on her?"

"Look at me, boy."

The sternness in Padre's voice drew Derin's attention immediately. Padre leaned forward, propping his elbows on his knobby knees.

"I don't see it." Padre sighed. "I know what you've been doing. Praying for years that you'd want something different. Then whatever happened last May, I've seen the change in you. That determination. Out of all Tres' kids, you've always been the most determined. When you set your mind to a thing, nothing deters you."

Derin allowed the words to settle for a moment. He had never seen himself as determined. He just did what had to be done. Whatever the moment called for, he did.

"Ever since your twin sister. Even then. When she passed, you never let her go."

"Twin sister?!" Derin's voice boomed across the patio as he straightened his back. Heat covered his face and neck as all eyes turned his direction. The faint scent of Mami's rose garden floated in the air as time seemed to slow. His heart pounded loudly in his ears.

"Elena."

Derin shook his head at his family, a grimace on his face. The old man's mind had to be fading. As he eased back against the chair, he reminded Padre of the truth, saddened by the old man's confusion.

"Elena was grandma's name. Your wife."

"Sure enough." Padre nodded slowly. "Tres named your twin after her."

Derin's heart galloped in his chest as his throat constricted. A twin. A sister. Not possible. Surely, he would have remembered her. Would have known someone was missing from his life.

"She died when you were toddlers. Not quite two years old. Before then, the two of you were inseparable." Padre gazed into the distance, his face softening. "Pretty little thing. Blond hair. Dark brown eyes. You held her hand a lot."

Padre snorted. "From the day you were born, you were watching out for her. Like you could sense she needed protection even then."

Derin could only stare at his grandfather as the words coming from his mouth made little sense. A tear trickled down the side of the old man's face, zigging and zagging in the deep wrinkles etched there. A gnarled finger swiped it away.

"When she died, it was one of the darkest days in this family's history. The two of you wandered off one afternoon. We found you both right before dusk. You were crying. Clutching her in your arms, rocking back and forth. None of us were sure how long she had been gone. Bit by a rattler, best we could tell."

Tears burned the back of Derin's eyes. He bit the inside of his cheek. Something floated in his memory just out of reach. But the overwhelming terror and grief assaulted him, feeling entirely too real. Like some part of him had been ripped away.

He bolted to his feet and shoved the back door open, knocking it hard against the wall. His eyes darted around the kitchen frantically until they landed on his Mami. He grabbed her arm and shuffled her into her room as his blood coursed like wildfire through his veins.

When he released her arm, he whirled to face her. Her wide eyes warned him to calm down.

"I had a sister?"

Derin choked on the question before sinking into the corner of his parents' bed. Elbows propped on his knees, his head dropped into his rough hands as unexplained pain tore through his soul like a raging monsoon. He had a sister. A twin sister that had died decades ago.

"Si, mijo." Mami's voice broke. "Elena. Named after your *abuela*."

"No." He shook his head. "No. This makes no sense."

"It's true, mijo."

Was this what was wrong with him? Was this why he used women? Longed to feel close to them, but pushed them away. No long-term attachments. A deep, decades old secret — could it explain it all?

He couldn't understand. Why had his parents kept this

from him?

"Who told you?"

Derin turned fierce eyes toward his mother. "Padre did. Why didn't you!"

"Mijo—"

"Don't!" he growled as he stood and darted around her. "I can't..."

Then Derin ran from the house, straight to his truck. He turned the key and sped away from the ranch—the house of lies and secrets—his heart dying a little with each mile.

MADISON'S GAZE SNAPPED to Derin's face as his outburst echoed across the patio. His twisted features broke her heart. Something bad had happened. She sensed it deep within her heart.

When he shook his head, most of his family picked up their conversation again. She felt torn. Clearly, something was wrong. As she watched him, the pain imprinted on his face deepened. He jumped up, storming into the house. A few minutes later, she heard the distinctive roar of his truck and she rushed through the house to the front porch in time to see the dust kick up behind his vehicle.

The urge to follow him felt strong. She must go to him. But how? He had driven her there.

A set of keys pressed into her palm, the metal cold against her skin.

"Go. Take my truck," River said. "Tacoma."

Madison hurried down the porch stairs, disarming the truck as she went. She climbed behind the wheel and backed out as quickly as she could. Then she followed fast behind Derin, the truck flying smoothly over the ruts in the dirt road. A dusty cloud billowed in her wake.

What had happened? Why was Derin running? Madison wasn't certain how she knew that's what he was doing.

As he drove past the resort, she breathed a sigh of relief. Prayers flooded her mind in disjointed fragments and she held on to the hope that the Spirit would intercede for both of them. For her to have the right words. For him to be safe and heal.

When Derin turned onto the asphalt of the highway, she followed, growing nervous as his speed edged higher than she preferred. She continued her pursuit, relieved when he finally pulled into the parking lot of a church—a different one than what his family attended.

The tires of his truck barked as he jerked it to a hard stop before cutting the engine. Madison parked nearby. She watched as Derin hunched over his steering wheel, shoulders shaking. She waited in the safety of River's truck, not sure what to do next or what had propelled her to follow him.

Derin sat up straight, then leaned his head back against the headrest. His lips moved animatedly, but she did not know what he said. Then he slammed his palm against the steering wheel before gripping it with both hands. Suddenly, his hands went limp and fell into his lap, his head leaning against the headrest again.

Madison waited and prayed. Prayed for him. Prayed for wisdom. She didn't want to invade his space if he needed the privacy.

Her phone pinged.

*You find him?* Sydney asked.

She sent back a message that he was alright and gave Sydney the address.

*Cole wants to know if he should come.*

*No. I think he needs to be alone.*

Sydney sent back a praying hands emoji.

Then Madison opened the Tacoma's door and slid

down. After shutting it, she armed the vehicle before she walked over to the passenger side of Derin's truck.

She took a deep breath and yanked the heavy door open. Then she eased into the seat and closed the door.

Derin turned red-rimmed blue eyes towards her. She held her arms open wide, and he accepted the comfort of her embrace, burying his face against her neck. Quiet sobs shook this powerful man's frame like an earthquake and its aftershocks. She held him close, offering wordless sympathy. His manly scent hung heavily in the air.

Madison wasn't sure how long they sat there, his grief dampening the shoulder of her dress. She would stay with him as long as he needed. Nothing besides his heart mattered in that moment as she rested her hand lightly over his soft hair.

When Derin finally released his hold, he looked away, straightening his back. He coughed a few times as his throat worked.

"Thank you." The words came out gruffly.

Madison captured his hand and held it, saying nothing.

Derin coughed again.

"Guess you're wondering what that was about."

She waited, allowing him as much time as he needed to share. He held her gaze when he spoke.

"I just learned I had a twin sister that died before our second birthday."

Tears burned her eyes as she listened to the entire story. How he thought his messed up view of women had probably come from this tragedy he couldn't even remember.

"I wish I could remember her. How awful is it I can't?"

"You were so young. I think it's normal not to remember things from such a young age."

"No one ever mentioned her. Not once. You'd think Dalton would have remembered her. He would have been six when we were born. Close to eight when she died. Even

Dylan probably remembered her."

"Maybe. Maybe not. Or they thought the memories were of your cousins."

Derin shook his head. "None of it makes sense."

After several minutes of silence, she spoke. "Do you want me to drive you home?"

Derin looked around the parking lot. "How did you get here, anyway?"

"River's truck."

He shook his head. "I can drive. She'll need her truck."

"Are you sure?"

He nodded. "Go. I'll head home and you can follow. Then I'll drive you back to the casita."

Once Madison returned to River's truck, Derin pulled out, and she followed him back to the ranch house. She dropped off River's keys before joining him in his truck. When he parked in front of the casita, she invited him in.

"No, thanks. I should go. My mother is probably waiting to hear from me."

"Okay. Tomorrow, I'll ride with Layla, Kevin, and Syd. It's alright if you don't make it."

Derin rubbed his hands over his face, groaning. Then he angled toward her.

"I'll be there, Madi. I promise."

She kissed him on the cheek before exiting his truck. Then she watched from the porch as he drove up the dirt road, out of sight.

As Madison entered the casita, she took a deep breath, overwhelmed with compassion for Derin. She sent up a few more prayers for him throughout the evening as she watched movies on the couch.

If he hadn't already stolen her heart before today, he certainly had now.

# 16

---

MADISON'S STOMACH CHURNED as Kevin drove her, Syd, and Layla to the charity tournament. Her day of reckoning.

The bright March sun caused her eyes to squint. She donned her sunglasses against the glare. The temperature lingered comfortably in the low-to-mid eighties, wrapping the day with a gentle warmth. Above, the sky stretched endlessly, unmarred by a single cloud, allowing the vibrant blue hue to dominate the scenery. It provided the ideal backdrop for an exhilarating tennis competition. One that would determine the course of her future.

Taking a deep breath, she exited the SUV, toting her gym bag. Syd and Layla followed behind her, while Kevin parked the vehicle. She hadn't been this nervous in a long time and suddenly she wished Derin had come with her instead of driving separately. He had offered, but she felt it made little sense for him to wait around with her for all the pregame photoshoots and registration.

A text pinged on her phone.

*You've got this, Madi.*

A smile stretched across her lips. Derin's text, followed by a dozen motivational gifs, warmed her to the core and took the edge off her nerves. If his texts were any sign, he seemed in good spirits today. Perhaps he had adjusted to the shocking news from the day before.

*Lord, I trust this day to You. Even though I don't know what Your plan is right now, I want it. I want to be as confident as the Vargases are about Your plan for my life. Give me the strength to face whatever comes today.*

"Ready?" Syd asked.

"No. Yes. Maybe."

"Shoulders back. Smile on," Kevin said.

Then he opened the door for Madison. She straightened her back and smiled, thinking of Derin's encouraging text. Cameras flashed in her face as she walked towards the locker room. Madison repeated Derin's words in her head. *You've got this, Madi.*

As soon as the door closed behind her, she sagged against the wall, grateful for the privacy. She closed her eyes and breathed the stale air of the locker room. Then Madison dropped her bag on a bench.

She retrieved her favorite tennis racket and made sure her backup was ready to go. In a tournament years ago, several strings broke during a match. Since then, she always carried a backup. Ironically, she hadn't needed one since.

"It's time to head to the courts," Syd said. She offered a sympathetic smile.

Madison handed her the gym bag and the extra racket. Then she followed Syd out to the courts. The bright blue of the modern court surface greeted her as she stepped into the sunlight. She enjoyed playing on the specially designed blue courts, made to enhance tennis ball visibility for televised games.

After twenty minutes of photos, including group shots and match ups, she thought her mouth might freeze in a smile. Her cheeks ached and her anxiety had returned.

With a quick glance over at the reserved seating, she saw Derin sitting there, waiting. When he noticed her looking his way, he tipped his dark brown cowboy hat, his fingertips grazing the brim. Warmth settled on her cheeks and she smiled, thankful he came to support her today.

The noise from the bleachers grew louder as more spectators filed in. She stretched out along the edge of the court, wincing at a pinch in her right shoulder.

"Need help?" Coach Layla asked. "Ryan showed me how to massage your shoulder."

Madison agreed as Sydney cleverly blocked the view of her from the TV cameras. The last thing she needed were the TV crews replaying it.

Finally, it was time to start the match. She grabbed her racket, twirling it twice before she headed to the net. They paired Madison with the third place finalist from the US Open—the one that Madison had forfeited because of her injury. She shook her opponent's hand before walking to the edge of the court. A slight breeze tickled her neck as she stretched her arm overhead. The crowd hushed as Madison tossed the bright yellow ball up in the air and whacked her racket down hard on the ball. It zoomed to the other side of the net, catching her opponent off guard for a split second before she sent the ball flying back toward Madison with a double-handed backhand.

With her next stroke, Madison scored a point. Her confidence grew with each return. She accumulated points at a fast clip, wondering if her opponent failed to warm up properly. Sweat beaded on her neck and trailed down her back. She could do this.

Suddenly, with little warning, her opponent sent the ball screaming just out of reach with an overhead smash. Madison dove for it. Sharp pain sliced through her injured shoulder as the ball flew out of bounds on her opponent's side. Instinctively, she dropped her racket and clamped her hand over her aching shoulder. Waves of nausea rolled over her with the intense pain—almost as fierce as the original injury. She sank to her knees as her eyes burned, the rough court surface chewing into her skin.

Her tennis career was over.

DERIN WOKE IN a foul mood from the lack of sleep after learning about his twin sister. Images from a sunny day in the desert, his little sister crying and convulsing before breathing her last breath, kept him tossing late into the night. He did not know if they were actual memories or his mind imagining what he had been told about her death.

He forced himself out of bed before showering and dressing in his favorite shirt and jeans. Madi needed him today. After the way she had been there for him yesterday, he would not fail her. He owed her.

Derin shoved his brown hat down on his head. As he walked to his truck, he texted Madi some encouraging words followed by a ridiculous number of animated gifs. A half-smiled kicked up one corner of his mouth. She would get a kick out of that.

As he drove toward The Phoenix Country Club, Derin prayed for peace — both for himself and for Madi. If he was honest with himself, he desperately wanted her to stay in Arizona. Except for her to do so would mean the end of her tennis career. And he could never wish that on anyone.

After he parked, he texted Syd to let her know he was there. She texted back instructions on where he should go to watch the first match. Madi had given the organizers his name for the reserved seating for family and friends.

Derin's heart picked up its pace when he glimpsed Madi posing for several photos. *Lord, please be with her today. Help her trust You for whatever comes.*

He wasn't sure exactly when he felt the deep connection he now shared with her. Somehow, over the course of the two months, they had grown very close. Maybe it was the one hundred and one questions. Or maybe God brought her to Vargas Sports so their paths would cross. Derin did not know, but he was thankful all the same.

When Madi looked his direction, he touched his fingertips to the brim of his hat. A soft smile played on her lips, causing her cheeks to blush that pretty rosy shade that he adored. Across the distance, their eyes locked for a few brief seconds. He hoped she read his undying support in them.

As the match began, Derin leaned forward, bracing his forearms on his legs. With Madi's first point, his fist pumped into the air. He pressed his lips into a firm line. He knew he had broken tennis etiquette. A vocal cheer would have been a serious breech.

He admired her athleticism as she continued to return the ball effortlessly. Several points into the match, he felt confident she would win it.

Until her opponent sent one zinging to the far corner of the court. His stomach clenched as Madi scurried toward it. *Let it go, Madi. It's too far.* He watched in horror as she whacked the ball in the air, overextending her right arm. Her racket fell from her hand right before she clutched her injured shoulder. She sank to the court, causing his heart to pound ferociously.

"Madi!"

Her name tore from Derin's lips as he vaulted over the end of the bleachers. The crowd collectively gasped as silence filled the tense air. The only sound was that of his boots clopping against the hard court as he ran toward the woman he loved. He had to protect her, save her from the coming storm.

"Madi."

He scooped her into his arms, hauling her to her feet. Then he took off his hat and blocked the view of her face. Her soft hair brushed against his arm as she leaned into his strength.

"I've got you."

"Derin." She sucked in a sharp breath and hissed it out through her teeth.

"I know, princess. It hurts. I've got you."

He quickened his pace as Layla walked on her other side. He noticed Layla's sharp shake of her head and his eyes traced her target. The security guard eased back. Within minutes, they were inside the privacy of the locker room.

Sydney skidded to a halt at the sight of Madi. She dropped her bag and rackets onto a bench. Then she rushed from the room, returning with a pack of ice.

"Here."

Madi accepted the ice, using the sling to cover her shoulder. Then Derin sat beside her, wrapping his arm loosely around her. She rested her head against his chest.

"I'm done. It's over." Madi choked on a sob, ripping Derin's heart from his chest.

He had no words to offer her. He understood she was right and he would not lie to her with empty platitudes. Instead, he rubbed his hand along her arm, letting her cry on his shirt.

When Derin looked up, he saw Layla's and Sydney's grim expressions. He would do anything to fix this for Madi. If only he could.

But he couldn't. The entire world would know today that Madison Moore's pro tennis career ended at the US Open in September. There was no coming back from this.

"Should we take her to the hospital? Madi, do you want to go?" he asked.

Her head nodded against his chest before she eased away from him.

"I should get an MRI. Might have torn it—" She choked. "Again."

"Do you want to go somewhere nearby, or do you want me to call Dr. Stone to see where she recommends?"

"Dr. Stone."

Derin called Dr. Stone as he walked out to his truck. Then he pulled around to a private entrance to the building, where Madi waited for him with Layla and Sydney. The crestfallen look on Madi's face chewed him up inside. Her dream shattered. He wanted to do whatever he could to smooth out this rough patch in her life. At that moment, it came as the opening of the door for Madi. When she struggled to fasten the seatbelt, he did it for her.

"Thanks," she whispered in a numb, surrendered tone.

Derin eased behind the wheel and drove to the hospital Dr. Stone recommended. She said she was on rotation that day and would come see Madi as soon as they arrived.

He turned on the radio to a country station, playing it softly in the background. Then he reached over and held Madi's hand, willing her to feel his support. Derin knew her heart ached. His did too.

# 17

MADISON BIT THE inside of her lip as she accepted the nurse's help to lean back on the MRI table. She shut her eyes tight as the table eased into the large white machine, willing the tears to stop.

Her career was over. Years of hard work. Physical conditioning. The hope of another Grand Slam vanished. Now, she presently hoped they could repair the damage to her shoulder. That she wouldn't suffer long-term issues because of it.

The tech's voice came over the speaker, explaining the test and the importance of remaining still. Madison hated the confining machine with its loud *cluck, cluck, pops*. Keeping her eyes shut, she tried to visualize something she loved. Usually, that would be tennis. But today, the image only brought pain.

Searching the reaches of her mind, the horse ride with Derin came to mind at last. His handsome blue eyes. Stocky build. That cocky grin he flashed right before teasing her. She wondered if he even knew he did that. She loved it. Loved him.

What would become of them? Did she even have the energy to figure it out, given the death of her pro tennis career?

When the tech told her she had a few seconds before the next test started, she breathed deeply and let it out slowly.

What would she do now?

Regardless of the outcome of the test, Madison's life would never be the same. There was no coming back from this. Not a second time.

Did she even want to?

Not really.

The hum and whir of the MRI sounded loud in her ears, despite the ear plugs. *Click, click, click, pop, pop.* The tech's muffled voice came over the speaker just seconds before the next round of imaging began. Madison forced her thoughts to something other than the present.

The memory of line dancing with Derin filled her mind's eye. The way his eyes lit up when she finally learned the new dance. Their laughter. Despite his past, Derin Vargas was a good man. He had captured her heart and enriched her life. She enjoyed the ranch, his home, and the man himself.

So what now? Did she go home to Colorado and help her parents? Stay here and make a life with Derin?

Too soon. Way too soon for thoughts like that. Madison didn't know if he wanted something permanent. She may have been nothing more than an experiment to him. To see if he could get to know a woman without crossing lines.

Ugh. She knew she meant more to him than that. Holding him in his truck yesterday, their deep connection solidified more. Derin respected her. Cared for her. Maybe he loved her.

"Madison, we're all done. Give us a second and we'll have you out of there."

The table jerked before it eased out of the machine. The nurse helped her sit up and asked her to wait a minute while the tech double checked the quality of the images. Soon enough, she was on her way to the waiting room.

"Madi."

Derin stood as soon as he saw her, crushing the brim of

his hat in his hands. Yeah, the cowboy cared deeply about her. It was clear from his hunched shoulders and furrowed brow that her well-being weighed heavily on his mind.

"When will you get the results?"

"Dr. Stone said she will call me as soon as she has them. She requested an expedited response, but it still might be a day or two. She couldn't tell from the physical exam if I tore it again or not."

Derin looped an arm around her, settling his hand on her waist. The sweet act comforted her more than she could say. Then he led her out to his truck.

On the drive back to Vargas Guest Ranch & Resort, her mind spun. Even if she hadn't torn her shoulder again, she ought to accept the end of her tennis career. The way it hurt, it seemed foolish to press on. No, she was done. No sense in delaying the inevitable.

"Do you have a place for press conferences at Vargas Sports?"

"Madi. Are you sure?" The pain in his voice mirrored the pain in her heart.

"My doctor back home warned me if I re-injured my shoulder or if I continued to have extreme pain, that I should consider my next steps carefully."

"If you're certain, I'll talk to Cole. When do you want to announce it?"

"Whenever you have a place ready."

Derin's warm, calloused hand wrapped around hers as she stared out the passenger window. Cacti whizzed by, reaching fat arms towards heaven, reminding Madison to lift her heart towards there too.

*Lord, please give me wisdom. Give me the words to say. Help me navigate what is next. Show me Your plan.*

She waited a few seconds, hoping for a sense of the future. None came. A loud breath expelled from her lungs. There would be no quick answers. No dramatic revelation.

Madison stole a glance at the cowboy next to her. She loved him. Loved life at Vargas Ranch. Deep in her heart, she knew what she had to do, despite wishing her reality could be different. She could stay for one more week before heading home to contemplate her future.

Leaving Derin and the ranch behind would hurt more than she wanted to admit.

TWO DAYS AFTER the charity tournament, Derin knocked on Madi's casita door. He waited several minutes before she finally opened it. Her eyes looked a little puffy, but they were dry. She wore a beautiful flowing top and jeans. Her golden locks hung straight—not the pretty curls he had grown accustomed to. Her slack face caused his heart to squeeze tight.

"Ready?" he asked.

Madi glanced away quickly, tears pooling in her eyes. She gave a sharp nod. He could practically feel her pain as if it was his own.

He had been with her when Dr. Stone called with the MRI results. Madi had a small tear that might require surgery in the future.

Derin escorted Madi to his truck and drove her over to the sports complex. Her manager and Cole decided the press conference ought to take place at the tennis court. Derin disagreed and nearly overruled them. He thought it heartless to make Madi give her retirement speech there. In the end, he capitulated.

It was the first press release at Vargas Sports, and it would be the one he remembered forever. Not because it was the first. His heart squeezed tight as he glanced over at Madi. She was the reason he would always remember it. Her sad eyes and hunched shoulders. The distant look in her gaze.

Madi let out a resigned sigh as he parked his dually. She shoved the door open before he could get it for her. Then she stalked toward the court, not waiting for him.

"Madi, wait!" He jogged to catch up to her, and she slowed her pace. "Do you want me to stand next to you?"

"No. That's not part of your responsibilities. Kevin will be there."

A knife sliced through him. She was pushing him away when he wanted to comfort her, care for her.

"Whatever you want," he ground out, fixing a scowl on his forehead.

As Derin started to walk away, Madi placed a hand on his arm. He stopped and turned toward her.

"I have to do this alone. Then you can take me out for lunch or whatever. Some place in town. Away from all..." She casually waved her hand in the air.

He nodded sharply before traipsing over to where Cole stood. He folded his arms over his chest, still hurt she wouldn't let him support her.

"Neutral face, Derin," Cole said. "Remember your official role."

Derin breathed deeply through his nose and let it out slowly, hoping it eased the tension on his face. He shook his hands out, letting them hang by his sides.

Camera lights flashed with their rapid-fire clicking echoing across the tennis court. Kevin stepped up to the podium and motioned for Madi to join him. He made a brief introductory statement before Madi took over amid another barrage of camera activity. Derin wondered how long it took to get used to the bursts of lights and sounds. Looking at Madi, he couldn't tell whether it bothered her.

She straightened her shoulders and placed her palms flat against the podium before she spoke.

"Thank you for coming. I would like to announce my retirement from pro tennis. I have enjoyed the amazing opportunity to play the sport I love for a long time. It is with a heavy heart that I leave. I appreciate the love and support of my family. To my fans, I'd like to say a special 'thank you.' You have been wonderful supporters for many years."

Kevin leaned forward to speak. "We'll take a few questions."

"Madison!" One reporter drew Kevin's attention, and he acknowledged her. "What will you do next? Will you return to your hometown?"

Derin watched as Madi struggled for emotional control. He wished she would have let him stand next to her, offering moral support. Despite not desiring his photo to be taken.

"I'm returning to my family's ranch in Colorado at the end of the week. I don't know where God will lead me."

Her announcement about going home caused Derin's gut to tighten. She hadn't told him she planned to leave in two days. He needed to know if she would continue their relationship. Or if she was leaving him behind.

Kevin took center stage again as Madi left the podium. She headed toward the parking lot, so Derin and Cole flanked her.

"Let's get out of here," she said, looking up at him.

Silently, he led her to his truck as his fears swirled. Perhaps she wanted nothing to do with him. Maybe she only used him as a distraction while she rehabbed at the ranch. Maybe she didn't trust him to change from his past. The ache in his heart splintered into a deep canyon.

When Derin parked in front of *The Lariat*, Madi waited for him to open the door this time. He breathed a little easier. Holding out his hand, his relief grew when she placed hers in it. Maybe they weren't done.

After they entered the building, he asked the owner for a

table in the back. He let her know if any media showed up, that he and Madi didn't want to be disturbed. The owner led them to a private table.

"I'm sorry, Derin," Madi said as soon as they sat down. "You probably have questions. I'm not sure if I have any answers."

He studied the menu for a minute, not really reading it, before setting it aside. "Are you really leaving in a few days?"

She released a loud breath. "Yes. I'm going home to my parents' ranch on Friday."

Two days. Derin rubbed sweaty palms on his pants. A deep ache spread through his chest. She was going to leave him. Just like the sister he didn't remember.

"Don't go. Stay here." With me.

Madi snorted. "And do what? I have no job. No way to pay for a room. Nothing here."

Derin leaned forward, frowning. "You have me."

Her gaze lowered to the menu.

"Madi, you mean too much to me to let you go without a fight. Stay."

Her eyes flashed as they connected with his. "I need some time to consider what I'll do with my life. The best place for me to do that is at home." She picked at the edge of the menu. "It's been a long time since I've seen my family."

After a server took their order, she returned a moment later with their beverages. Derin sipped on his soda. Madi's gaze darted everywhere except to him. He felt her pulling away. This was it. The only woman he had ever loved was going to leave him.

Madi's shoulders rose and fell. Then she finally looked at him.

"It's not you."

He snorted. How many times had he been the one saying those words? More than he could count.

"I just need time to figure out my next steps."

The server returned, placing their sandwiches in front of them.

Derin extended his hand, counting his heartbeats until Madi placed her hand in his. He bowed his head and prayed for the food.

After he ate a few bites of his sandwich, he asked, "Are you breaking up with me?"

Madi set her sandwich down. "I don't know."

He frowned. "You don't know? Do you love me or not, Madi?"

"That's not fair. We've only known each other for a few months."

"And I love you." There. She would have to stay now. "Derin?"

He growled as his head whipped toward the familiar feminine voice. A woman with a baby in a stroller waved at him. Then recognition dawned.

"Nicole."

His stomach lurched, and he coughed as he launched to his feet. He held up a finger to Madi.

"Give me a minute. I'll be right back."

Derin missed her response as he shuffled Nicole a few feet away. His throat constricted. Through clenched teeth, he asked, "What do you want?"

"I thought you might like to meet your son."

His blood boiled. No way was the kid his. His eyes darted to the baby as doubt niggled. No way. Not possible. He had taken precautions. Just what game did the vicious cougar have up her sleeve?

"I don't believe you," he spat out.

"Look, he's got your eyes."

Derin leaned over the stroller. Sure enough, the baby had blue eyes. But, then again, so did the baby's mother.

"That proves nothing."

"Why won't you believe me?"

Derin growled. "Because you lied to me before. Kinda sorta forgot to mention your husband. Considering you were with more than one man back then, I doubt very much the kid is mine."

Besides, he had always been careful. Used protection. Even if the woman claimed to be on the pill, like Nicole had. Clearly, that had been a lie too.

When Nicole started to say more, Derin interrupted. "You and your kid have no place in my life. You need to leave."

# 18

---

MADISON COUGHED TO hide her shock. Before that moment, she had considered a long-distance relationship with Derin.

His confession from a month ago came to her mind. He had been with "more than a dozen" women. This Nicole person had clearly been one of them, judging by Derin's frowns directed at the baby in the stroller.

Is this what life with Derin would be like? A series of random women claiming he fathered their children?

Her stomach churned, her sandwich turning sour in it. She slid her plate away. Madison wanted to run out of there, leaving Derin Vargas far behind. Except he was her ride.

Madison listened as the two argued for a moment before Derin finally convinced the woman to leave.

When he sat down again, he apologized. "I'm sorry about that—"

"Sorry you have a son?" The acidic question bolted from her lips before she thought better of it.

"He's not mine."

"How do you know?" She captured her lower lip between her teeth.

Derin let out a long sigh. Then he reached for her hand. She pulled away.

"Madi, please don't judge me. I know the child isn't

mine. I was always very careful."

She crossed her arms over her chest. "You said she was married. How many married women have you been with?"

"Just Nicole. Only because she lied about it."

Madison narrowed her eyes at him. She didn't know what to believe. Despite how much she cared for him, she didn't trust him. Could never trust him. Not with this latest revelation.

"Take me home."

"Madi, please—"

"I'm done talking. Take me back to the casita. I need to pack."

As his shoulders slumped, she rose to her feet and stalked toward the door. Once outside, she straightened her back. The ache in her chest would dim in time. She needed to break it off with Derin. Forget about him. Forget about Vargas Ranch and the amazing family. Ignore the dreams that had bloomed in her heart.

His truck beeped, letting her know he had disarmed it. Madison yanked the door open and climbed into the passenger seat, bolstering her resolve with each movement.

The cab filled with a strenuous silence. She looked out the window, willing the minutes to pass quickly.

Derin Vargas was not the man for her. He used women. Had probably used her, too, even though they never crossed *that* line. Besides, she had no place for a man in her upended life. She had big decisions to make about her future.

The moment he parked in front of the casita, she darted out of the massive vehicle.

"Madi, wait! Can we please talk?"

"It's over, Derin. Forget about me. Move on with your life. It's what I'm going to do."

Then she entered the casita, letting the door slam shut. She angled toward the window with a view of his truck. He stood staring at the door for a solid minute. Her heart raced, still clinging to a glimmer of hope, until he spun on his heel. When he peeled out of the parking lot, she ran down the hall to her room, tears raining down her face as she went.

She would never forget Derin Vargas, no matter how hard she tried. She loved him.

FRIDAY MORNING, MADISON wheeled her luggage to the casita's porch. Kevin slung them into the trunk of the rented SUV. The resounding *thud* echoed like the death of her heart. Every personal and professional dream crumbled at the sound.

She turned back to Sydney, another source of heartache. Blinking back tears, she said, "I'm going to miss you. Did you decide what's next for you?"

"I'm going to stay here. There's a room at the women's housing. Cole is still talking about a job for me with Derin. If that doesn't pan out, then I'll head back to my parents."

Madison swiped her damp cheek before hugging her friend. "Thank you for everything—especially your friendship."

"You're almost like a sister." Sydney squeezed her before backing away. "Are you sure you won't reconsider a relationship with Derin? He loves you, Madison."

Madison looked toward the gravel path leading to the sports complex, eyes stinging. "I can't."

"Sorry. I didn't mean to…"

"Stay in touch, Syd."

"I will."

Madison pivoted toward the SUV's passenger seat. "Let's go, Kevin."

On the trip to the airport, the two barely spoke until they neared the departures. They said their farewells, and Madison thanked him for his years of service. Then she checked her bags before making her way to her gate.

The flight from Phoenix to Durango only took about an hour and a half. As it descended onto the runway, Madison studied the western slope of the Rockies. The mountains looked unfamiliar. Yet, she had grown up with them standing guard to the east of her home near Bayfield. When the plane landed and she descended the stairs, the peace she hoped she would find still eluded her. Perhaps it would come once at home.

The cold air pricked her skin, a stark reminder of Colorado's wintery climate. She hurried inside the terminal, searching for her parents.

"Madison!" Her brother's voice called her name.

"Mason?"

He engulfed her in a brotherly bear hug. "You look too tan to come to Colorado."

She giggled.

"You remember Cammie Yardley?"

Madison noticed as Mason slid his arm around Cammie's waist. Thankfully, Mom had warned her about her brother's girlfriend. "Nice to see you."

Cammie smiled and greeted Madison. Mason ushered them toward baggage claim as Cammie chattered. Madison only half listened, her heart still back in Arizona. Her mind stuck on a handsome cowboy. Surely, the heartache would fade in time.

When there was a break in the conversation, she shot off a text to Syd, letting her know she landed safely. She had almost texted Derin, too. Almost.

"You seem distracted," Cammie said as Mason tossed her luggage in the back seat of his extended cab dually. Not so different from Derin's.

"Just have a lot on my mind."

"Understandable," Mason said. "If I had to guess, you

have given little thought to life after tennis."

"Understatement of the year."

Mason held the door open for her. She climbed onto the seat next to her suitcase. Then buckled in.

Cammie and Mason spoke in soft tones, thankfully leaving Madison to her troubled thoughts. It would be good to be on the ranch again. See her other brother and her parents. Give her heart a chance to heal, along with her shoulder.

If only she could stop thinking about the man who stole her heart.

DERIN STOOD IN the lawyer's office, glaring at Nicole. It had taken a week of curt phone calls to convince her to consent to a paternity test for her son.

Not once had Derin allowed the doubt to take over. He knew the kid wasn't his. Still, he needed the lab results to confirm it so he could say goodbye to the lying woman.

"I have the results," his attorney said. "There is no familial connection between Derin and your son."

Nicole didn't even have the decency to act surprised. He bit back all kinds of bad words to describe her. She had known he wasn't the father.

When she started to say something, Derin stormed out of the attorney's office. He had had enough of her lies. With nothing to tie him to her, he could walk away. So he did.

Too bad Nicole had ruined his last conversation with Madi. If she hadn't, would he have convinced Madi to stay?

He shook his head as he climbed into his truck and drove back to work. When he parked in his reserved spot, he stared at his phone. He tapped on Madi's contact and stared at their messages.

Not a single word passed between them for two excruciating weeks. Derin's thumb hovered over the keyboard. He quickly typed out: *Thinking of you. Hope the time with your family is good.*

He wanted to tell her he wasn't Nicole's son's father. He wanted to ask her another dozen of the one hundred and one questions. More than that, he wanted to ask her to come home. Work with him at Vargas Sports.

A tap on his window drew his attention. Cole stood there. Derin stuffed his phone into his shirt pocket and exited his truck.

"Everything ready?"

Cole nodded. "Just didn't want to start without you."

Derin headed towards the sports complex, to the conference room. Five men sat around the conference room table. Adan Franco shot him a grin before taking his seat. Then he opened the meeting with a prayer.

Despite trying to focus on the prayer, Derin's mind offered a different one. That God would bless the Bible study for the athletes visiting Vargas Sports.

When "amens" sounded around him, Derin lifted his gaze. Herc Malvoy listened with rapt attention to Adan as he read the passage about Peter walking on water. The other athletes, mostly football players, followed along on their phones.

Adan showed a picture on the conference room TV.

"Most artists depict this scene with Peter reaching out to Jesus while he is still above water."

Then he displayed a different picture. Peter was underwater, sinking deeper, finally looking up at Jesus's hand as He plunged it beneath the surface.

"You might actually feel like this right now. Sinking in doubt. Overwhelmed by the lack of clarity for your future. Will you play next season? Will your damaged body regain enough strength to make it possible? Or will your career end? Has it already ended and you just haven't realized it yet?"

The men shifted in their chairs. Derin rubbed a hand over his heart, dealing with similar overwhelming feelings.

"You might not even realize that your head has slipped beneath the surface of the water. You may feel you are reaching for Jesus, but He's not answering."

Adan's gaze connected with each man, one at a time. "Look at this picture again. Who is doing the reaching?"

Then Derin saw it, flipping the script on everything he thought he knew about this passage.

Herc blurted out, "Jesus. Jesus is reaching beneath the surface to bring Peter out of the water."

"Exactly," Adan said. "Even when we think we're doing everything right—seeking His direction for our lives—we may see things wrong. We may miss how He is working."

A verse from Romans came to Derin's mind. "He works all things together…"

"For the good of those who love him," Adan said.

"And are called according to his purpose," Herc finished the verse.

"When I faced ending my pro bull riding career," Adan said. "I couldn't discern His purpose in it. I knew that verse and believed it. But I hadn't walked through it. I hadn't come out the other side of a pivotal life-changing circumstance to truly understand that even in the storm—even sinking beneath the surface—it was all part of His plan. A plan I wasn't meant to see until later."

"There's a purpose in the waiting." Herc's eyes lit with understanding. "Even during this time, there's a purpose."

Derin cleared his throat. "And that's what we hope to help you with. We offer opportunities to serve in the equine therapy program my brother Dylan runs."

"Equine therapy?" one athlete asked.

Adan explained the purpose of Braden's Hope, the charity he co-founded with Dylan. How they helped disabled children experience the joy of horseback riding. And how they thought the athletes might benefit by helping the kids.

"It sounds amazing," Herc said.

Derin listened as Adan answered their questions. Each man seemed happier, eager to help. Exactly what he had hoped would happen. Get them to see beyond their problems. Give God time to work in their lives and through their injuries.

Now, if only God would do the same for Derin.

# 19

MADISON SNUGGLED DEEPER under the covers, not thrilled about waking before dawn to face the cold outdoors. She had been away from Colorado for too long. Her blood had thinned, spending so much time in mild, inviting climates. Even after three weeks back home, she could not get warm.

She sighed and tossed back the covers before quickly stuffing her feet into fuzzy slippers. She donned a thick robe as a shiver slithered down her back. Ugh.

The smell of bacon, sausage, and coffee wafted toward her as she neared the kitchen. When she first arrived back home, Mom told her she was too skinny. Madison tried her best not to overindulge on the rich food Mom served. Bacon every day was bound to add a few pounds to her waistline.

"Need help?" Madison asked as she poured herself a mug of coffee. She dumped some flavored creamer into the dark liquid before sipping it. Slowly, it warmed her from the inside out.

"Oh, no. You relax," Mom answered.

She snorted. "I've spent too much time relaxing. I need to figure out what I'm gonna do with my life."

Mom raised an eyebrow before turning her attention back to the stove. She used tongs to flip the bacon over, cooking it for another minute. Then she plated it. Taking a dozen eggs, she cracked them into the hot pan, whisking them over the heat. It had always marveled Madison how Mom could do that without the scrambled eggs half cooking. She gave up trying years ago, opting to scramble them in a bowl first.

With a giant silicon spatula, Mom folded the fluffy eggs before removing the skillet from the heat. She scraped them into a bowl right as the back door opened, bringing in a gust of frigid air, along with Madison's brothers and father.

"Perfect timing," Dad said as he ambled toward Mom. He placed a kiss on her cheek as she set the large platter of bacon and sausage on the table.

Mason and Micah toed off their boots and hung their coats on the hooks in the mudroom. Dad offered grace before passing food around the table.

"You eat like a bird," Micah, her oldest brother, teased.

Madison rolled her eyes. "I'm not exercising hours a day. I don't want to gain forty pounds."

"Spend the day out on the ranch and you'll change your mind," Mason said.

"What, and deprive you of work?"

"There's plenty to go around," Dad said.

Madison frowned and picked at her tiny pile of scrambled eggs. She stood and retrieved some apple slices from the fridge, nibbling on one as she sat down. It was hard to get used to hearty ranch food again.

"We could use some extra hands today. The weather service warns a winter storm is coming in a few days," Micah said.

Madison agreed to help. While the men inhaled their food, she studied Micah. He had grown up while she was gone. It surprised her when he gave the weather report—something Dad used to do. He seemed to embrace stepping into the ranch manager role. At thirty-three, he had plenty of experience.

Her gaze shifted to her dad. A few streaks of dark brown broke up his silver hair. Covered in leathered skin, his rough hands told the story of a life spent working on the ranch. Wrinkles formed deep lines near his eyes and his cheeks. Mom sported her fair share of gray hair and wrinkles, too. Her parents were aging.

The back door opened. Madison glanced over her shoulder, surprised to see Cammie.

"Sorry I'm late."

Mason scooted the chair next to him away from the table. Cammie eased into it.

"You know if you married her," Micah teased, "She wouldn't have a ten-mile drive every morning."

Mason's cheeks flamed red while Cammie ducked her head. Then she flashed her left hand under the light. A small round diamond sparkled against a yellow gold band.

Madison grinned, happy for her brother.

"He asked last night if you must know."

Dad reached over and squeezed Mason's shoulder. Mom offered a grin, along with her congratulations. Micah did too.

"Congratulations," Madison said. "When is the wedding date?"

Cammie glanced at Mason. "We were thinking of flying over to Vegas in a few weeks."

"No church wedding?" Mom asked.

Mason clasped Cammie's hand on the table. "We don't want a big fuss. The four of you know. That's plenty."

Madison watched as Cammie's smile faded, and she looked down. She knew about Cammie and her sister's home life. No surprise she wouldn't want to share the news with her dad. No one had seen her mom in decades.

"We can still have a small ceremony in the church," Mom said.

"I'll... Think about it."

Madison's thoughts drifted to Derin. If she had stayed with him, would he have proposed? Would she be planning a June wedding?

The thought caused the food in her stomach to sit like a rock. She pushed her plate away and excused herself to dress for the day. Then she rode out to the herd with the men.

"Awfully quiet today, sis."

Madison pulled her warm scarf down, resting it below her chin. "I'm happy for you and Cammie."

"I'm not talking about me. Something is up with you. More than just the end of your tennis career."

She shrugged.

"You met someone, didn't you?"

She had said nothing about Derin since returning home. Her eyes stung, and not from the cold.

"Derin Vargas."

"From the rehab place?"

She nodded.

"What happened?"

Madison sucked in a deep breath, the icy air pricking her lungs. Then she told him about her whirlwind months with Derin.

"Sounds like you love him."

"I don't know." She left out the part about Derin's past. And his baby's mama.

The thought stabbed her guilt. Syd had texted her the paternity test proved the baby wasn't his. Still, he had been with the baby's mother. And many, many more women.

But he had not lied about that. He confessed it, first to God, then to her. If God forgave Derin, why couldn't she?

A heifer dashed away from the herd on Mason's side. "Hup. Hup." He rode toward her, easing her back to the herd.

Madison felt numb inside. Frozen in place and not from

the chilly Colorado April. She was stuck in limbo. No matter how hard she tried, she could not forget Derin Vargas or his family or their amazing business. She wanted to be a part of what they were doing there.

Should she call him and ask for a job?

She shook her head. He wouldn't want to see her or work with her. Not after the way she callously tossed his heart aside.

Once they moved the herd to the fenced pasture, Madison rode to the stable, grateful for the warmth of the enclosed building. She cared for her horse before heading inside.

Then she helped her mom fix dinner.

"Something is on your mind."

It should not surprise her that Mom could tell.

"Just thinking about my bossy cowboy."

Mom laughed. "You fell in love with this bossy cowboy?"

"Yeah. Hopelessly."

Then she told Mom about Derin telling her what to do on the tennis court. The one hundred and one questions. The line dancing. Picnics. Cowboy church. His family.

"He sounds perfect for you. Why are you still here?"

"To help you all."

Mom laughed. "I've loved spending time with you, Madison, but your heart isn't in Colorado."

No, it wasn't. It was on Vargas Ranch outside of Wickenburg, Arizona.

"I'll pray for you to have clarity and wisdom."

"Thanks, Mom."

"Now, would you mind setting the table?"

DERIN STARED AT the reservation system on his browser. For the tenth day in a row, he typed in the request for airline tickets to Durango, Colorado. He selected a one-way flight and stopped right before clicking the purchase button.

A noise from the doorway of his office drew his attention. He quickly closed the browser before lifting his gaze.

"Morning, Derin," Sydney greeted him.

He motioned her to enter.

"Just wanted to make sure you saw the schedule for the men's Bible study, counseling, and equine therapy."

"Yeah. Great job figuring all that out."

"Oh, it was my pleasure. I love seeing how each of the programs helps the athletes here."

"Any luck finding a leader for the women's Bible study yet?"

Sydney stepped deeper into the office as her eyes dropped to the back of one guest chair. She rested her hands lightly on it.

"About that." Her gaze met his. "I have the perfect candidate. Female athlete recently retired from her career. Strong Christian. Loves Arizona. Loves this ranch."

Derin's stomach knotted as his chest squeezed tight.

"She just needs you to offer her the job."

"Sydney —"

"Hear me out. She loves you, you know. I hear it in her voice when she asks about you."

Madi asked about him?

"Then why doesn't she text me back?"

"She's scared, Derin."

Cole entered. "Am I interrupting?"

He slung an arm around Sydney, causing Derin to wonder when Cole would propose. They were perfect together.

"I was just suggesting Derin hire Madison."

"You should. In fact, fly up there today."

"Today?"

Cole chuckled. "Come on. I've caught you at least twice trying to book a flight to Durango."

"I don't have her address." Derin stalled. He knew how to fix that.

Sydney pulled her phone out of her pocket and tapped a few times before Derin's phone buzzed.

"Problem solved."

Derin glanced at the message. Madison's contact, complete with address, cell phone, and her parents' number at the ranch.

"What are you waiting for?" Cole asked.

"What if she doesn't want me?"

Sydney laughed. "I told you, she loves you. She'll come for you and the job."

Derin frowned.

Syndey's thumbs flew across her phone screen. His pinged again.

"Better hurry, boss. Your flight leaves in two and a half hours."

He opened the message. Airline reservations from Phoenix to Durango.

"Go. And pack for a week. Cole said he'd give you the time off."

Derin snorted. "Who's the boss again?"

"I'll reserve a car for you, too. Expect another text."

"Thanks, Sydney."

Derin hurried out to his truck and drove home. He borrowed a suitcase from Dalton, shoving several changes of clothes into it.

His mind whirred as he drove to the airport. What would Madi say? It seemed silly to offer her a job just to lead a women's Bible study two days a week. That wasn't a job. It was a ploy to get her to move home to where she belonged. With him.

A real job would take more than a few hours per week.

Perhaps she could lead trail rides for the athletes. Mentor and befriend them, kinda like a transition coach. Someone to guide them through some decisions they needed to make for life after sports. Yeah, the transition coach sounded like a great fit. He knew Madi would bring her own ideas and develop it beyond his initial vision.

Most importantly, she would move to Arizona. Live on Vargas Ranch. Be close so they could resume their relationship. Then, he would propose. Ask her to be his wife. Because no other woman would ever be right for him.

Derin parked his truck in short-term parking, not caring about the cost. Then he grabbed his suitcase and hurried into the terminal building, carefully following the signs for ticketing check-in. Thank goodness Cole texted him a few notes about how to navigate air travel, as it was the first time Derin had ever flown.

After checking his bags, he made his way through security. His face heated when he forgot to remove his belt with its giant buckle, and the security agent asked him to do so. Once through security, he only had to wait at the gate for a few minutes before boarding began.

He ducked as he entered the plane, feeling confined already. The narrow aisle barely left an inch on either side of his hips. He tried not to hit anyone with his broad shoulders. He stuffed himself into the seat, if one could call the teeny thing a seat. It felt like he had to tuck his knees up around his ears.

When the plane careened down the runway, Derin gripped the armrest tightly. As it lifted into the air, his stomach floated for a few seconds before it settled back in its proper place. He breathed deeply before letting it out slowly. Not too bad. He could learn to enjoy flying, not that he wanted to leave the ranch much.

What was he doing? Flying to Madi. What if she didn't want to see him? What if she sent him packing?

*Pray.*

Right. Derin allowed his soul to lift to the Father who knew all things. He asked for the words to say. He asked for Madi's heart to soften. Above all, he asked for God's plan to come to fruition.

*I do not deviate from the Lord's plan.*

An hour and a half later, Derin stepped onto the tarmac. The icy wind prickled his exposed arms. Yeah, he needed a coat ASAP. When he entered the terminal, he rubbed his hands along his arms. While he waited for his bag, he searched for the closest box store since the airport had little in the way of shops.

With bag in hand, he hurried to the car rental building. The clerk had compassion on him and offered him a puffer coat from their lost and found.

"It's been here for four months. I don't think the owner is going to claim it."

The clerk slid the key across the counter.

"You should be on your way soon. Winter storm is coming through tonight."

"Thanks."

Derin stuffed his arms in the puffer, pleased that it fit well enough. Then he found the world's smallest car. A Prius. He opened the door and shoved the seat back as far as it would go before turning it on. He stowed his suitcase in the back seat. Then he folded his long legs into the tiny space. His head brushed the top of the interior, so he angled the seat back. Sheesh. This must be what a sardine felt like.

Oh well. Madi was worth an uncomfortable hour's drive in a minuscule car.

He pulled out, heat blasting, as the navigation on his phone told him where to go. The further into the mountains he went, he lost the signal. Snow began to fall. With wipers frantically whipping back and forth over the windshield, Derin prayed for a safe journey. And that he wouldn't get lost.

And that Madi would say yes.

# 20

MADISON HAD FELT restless all day. She had debated in her mind for days about flying down to Arizona. Asking Derin for a job. Not that she knew what she was qualified to do.

Standing in front of the frost-covered window, she wished once again for a college degree, longing for the opportunities it would bring. The snowfall intensified, with huge snowflakes rapidly accumulating on top of the existing inches from the previous week. It was so heavy she could barely see the twinkling lights lining the drive.

The warmth of a person next to her drew her thoughts back to the moment.

"It's really coming down now," Dad said. "Glad we finished the chores early."

"Yeah, I wouldn't want to be out in that," Micah said.

Her either. She sighed heavily, letting the curtain drop back in place before sitting in front of the cozy fire.

"Wait, was that a car?" Micah asked, sweeping the curtain back from the window.

"Yeah," Dad said. "A tiny white thing. Skidding all over the drive."

"I'll go check it out," Micah said.

Madison joined her dad at the window again. A Prius slid from one side of the drive to the other, inching slowly closer. The headlights blinded them from seeing the person driving. Micah jogged through the shin-high snow toward the determined vehicle. It skidded to a stop, fish tailing at the end. A huge, broad-shouldered man exited the itty-bitty car.

"Derin?"

His name fell from her lips in a breath as he placed his cowboy hat on his head. Micah spoke to the man — maybe it wasn't Derin. Then the man leaned in, turned off the car, and retrieved a suitcase.

As he strode toward the house, next to Micah, the porch light shone on his bearded face. It was him.

Before a thought formed, Madison flung the door wide and ran down the porch stairs, stocking clad feet and all. The closer she came to him, she saw his surprise. Then she launched herself into his embrace, his powerful arms encircling her. The spicy scent of his cologne brought a flood of emotion to her heart. She had missed him more than she realized.

"Derin! You're here!"

His deep chuckle sent thrilling tingles through her as he spun her around in the falling snow.

"Come on in. Madison, you'll catch your death of a cold!" Mom called from the open front door.

Derin swept her into his arms, carrying her up the porch stairs and depositing her inside the entryway.

She couldn't believe it. Derin was here.

"Madison, go change out of your wet clothes while we welcome your guest."

She didn't want to leave him. Her eyes sought his, and he gave an almost imperceptible nod. Madison hurried to her room, changing into fresh socks and flannel pants and shirt. Then she pounded down the stairs, stopping short of hugging Derin again.

"Mom, Dad, this is Derin Vargas."

"We know, honey. He introduced himself. Why don't you fix him some hot cocoa?"

"I'll help," Cammie said. She had been staying in one of the guest rooms since Mason didn't want her stranded at her dad's place in the winter storm.

"Who's the handsome cowboy?"

Madison's hands shook as she filled the kettle with water and set it on the stove to boil. She gave Cammie the highlights.

"We dated while I was in Arizona."

"So he's your boyfriend?"

"I wouldn't call him that. We broke up before I left."

Cammie snorted. "He's here. I think that means he's still your boyfriend."

Madison's heart raced. Cammie was right. Derin must love her to fly—oh, it was his first time! She had forgotten. He flew in an airplane for her.

"Oh, my."

Cammie smiled before she turned to the cupboards to retrieve six mugs. Then she emptied packets of hot cocoa mix with marshmallows into each one. When the kettle whistled, Madison poured the water into the mugs. They stirred the cocoa before placing the mugs on a tray. Madison's hands shook too much, so Cammie carried the tray. She set it on the coffee table.

"What are you doing here?" Madison finally asked when she settled onto the couch next to her man.

He winked at her. "I came to take you back to Arizona."

"Still bossy, I see."

"Come on, you know you like it."

Madison smiled at him over the rim of her mug.

"Truth be told, I came to offer you a job. But seeing you now..."

Derin set his mug on the end table. He took hers from her hands and set it next to his before he pulled her to her feet. Then he dropped to one knee.

"Madison Moore, these last few weeks without you have felt empty. I'm lost without you. Will you be my plus one on a deserted island? Will you walk by my side? I love you more than anything—enough to brave an airplane for the first time. To drive in a sardine can amid a Colorado winter storm."

Madison's heart pounded loudly in her ears. Was he asking her to marry him?

DERIN SWALLOWED HARD as his neck craned back to see Madi's eyes. The words flowing from his mouth hadn't been what he planned to say. Nor when he planned to say it.

When she came running from her parents' home, blond hair whipping in the wind, he knew beyond any doubt; he wanted her as his wife. He didn't need more time to decide. His heart had bonded with hers over the last few months. He had one hundred and one reasons to love her forever.

So his heart took over. He dropped to his knee, despite not having a ring in his pocket. He declared his love to his Madi.

Except she hadn't said a word in response. Did she not love him after all?

His throat constricted. He forced more words out.

"I want to give you that perfect morning. Sunlight streaming through the windows. Kids jumping on us. I want to be the man you wake up next to for the rest of our lives."

Tears trailed down her cheeks. She nodded at last.

Derin bolted to his feet, pulling her against his chest.

"Yes, Derin." Her muffled reply soothed his fear as she leaned back to look into his eyes. "I will be your plus one on a deserted island. I'll be the woman you wake up next to."

A smile quirked one side of her lips.

"I won't even make you watch that terrible end-times movie or bad remakes of movies made in the eighties."

"I love you, Madi."

"I love you, Derin. Now kiss me."

"Hey, I thought I was the bossy one."

His Madi pulled his face close, and he kissed her soundly, despite her entire family watching.

"Guess that means we've got two weddings coming up," her father teased.

Slowly, Derin released his fiancée. Her family congratulated them. Then they offered him a guest room on the opposite side of the house from hers. Didn't matter. He would wait for his wedding night. He loved Madi too much not to be patient.

MADISON GRINNED AS Derin held the door of the dining hall open. Then he held her hand, the one with the big sparkly rock he bought her in Durango before they boarded the plane this morning. Scanning the crowd, a sense of belonging washed over her. This was home.

The Vargas family sat at the long table in the private room of the dining hall. Derin carried her full plate for her while she carried their beverages. Then they sat at the table. Tres Vargas offered a heartfelt prayer before Madison joined the family to end the prayer.

"We do not deviate from the Lord's plan."

She loved their motto. It anchored her in the biggest storm of her life. And it paved the way for her to open her heart to Derin and to a new life apart from tennis. Vargas Ranch truly felt like home.

As the meal wound down, Derin stood, gathering everyone's attention.

"Madison has agreed to take a job at Vargas Sports."

She hid her smile behind her hand, knowing he planned to build toward the big announcement.

"She's going to be a transition coach and Bible study leader for the athletes."

His family congratulated them. Still, Derin stood there next to her.

"Is there more, son?" Tres asked.

"Si," Catalina said. "Something to do with the ring?"

Derin's face turned red. "Madison has agreed to marry me."

Catalina squealed and rounded the table, pulling Madison into her arms. "Another bonita mija."

Madison smiled. She appreciated Catalina's exuberant acceptance.

As the congratulations settled, Madison spoke up. "We'd like to marry in June. After Dalton and River return from Hawaii."

"She'll be sharing Sydney's room in the women's housing until then," Derin said.

"Who wants empanadas?" Drake asked, bringing the festive feeling back to the gathering.

As the family agreed it was time for dessert, Derin leaned closer. "I can hardly wait for June. But I will."

Madison giggled. "I guess even bossy cowboys can learn to compromise."

"It's six weeks away, Madi. Doesn't feel like much of a compromise, compared to a lifetime with you."

He nipped at her ear, and she leaned away. "Patience, cowboy."

Derin winked at her as he slid his arm off her shoulders. Then he dug into the empanada.

Who knew when she arrived at Vargas Guest Ranch & Resort back in January that she would find the love of her life, a new career, and a place to call home? God did. He had a plan all along. One for her good. For Derin's good. And for the good of other athletes walking through the storms of life.

"What?" Derin asked.

"I love it here, Derin. And I love you."

Derin waggled his eyebrows and planted a honey sweet kiss on her lips. She thanked God for bringing her to him and helping her to trust her bossy cowboy for the rest of her life.

# Epilogue

_____

DEVON VARGAS GLANCED at his normally overconfident older brother. Derin had been a nervous wreck for two days. Having watched his other two older brothers fall in love, Devon figured love messed with a man's brain.

He wouldn't know. Had never come close to falling for a woman. Sure, he dated a little here and there. Enjoyed a dinner out or a movie. Nothing too deep.

He didn't have time for love. He was still finishing up his degree. By this time next year, he would finally finish his Master's. Finally, be able to teach high school history.

For years, he worked late into the night to complete first his Bachelor's degree and now his Master's. During the day, he ran the children's program. If only he could keep a children's director on staff. Then he could pursue his dreams off the ranch. Take that missions trip to Guatemala to work with a kids ministry. Teach history next fall. Maybe even find an apartment in town. Or in Phoenix.

The demand for qualified teachers never ended. Many left the profession after a few years. It was hard work, but Devon understood hard work. Wasn't afraid of it. In some ways, he thought having just one job would seem easy after years of working on the ranch, going to college, and running the children's programming at the resort. Yeah, one job, forty hours a week—even sixty—would feel like a breeze compared to his life now.

He smiled as he led some of Madison's extended family to the bride's side of the church. He was happy for Derin and Madison. Despite Derin's questionable past with women, it made Devon proud to watch Derin transform into a solid Christian man, fully committed to the woman he chose for his wife. They were a perfect match, or so Mami said.

Devon didn't know. He had no time for dating, love, or a family of his own. Maybe one day he would change his mind. It just wouldn't be in the next few years.

The wedding ceremony seemed to go fast. Derin had chosen him as the best man. Seemed each older brother chose the next in line. That unintentional tradition would probably end today. Devon fully expected Drake to fall in love and marry long before Devon was ready to settle down.

When the pastor told Derin he could kiss his bride, the wedding guests silenced. Devon had wondered if Derin would go with a wild kiss, or sweet and tender. It was hard to predict anything about Derin.

Devon smiled when it looked like Derin hesitated. Madison placed her hands on her husband's cheeks and she started the kiss, sweet as it appeared. Guess they had all lost that bet. Not that any of them gambled.

At the reception, Devon hung around the outskirts, his usual approach to big events. He liked people-watching. Like now. Madison's mom and dad smiled non-stop. They watched as Derin and Madison danced, unaware of the world around them.

Devon wondered what about a woman could command a man's undivided loyalty and devotion. The entire notion perplexed him. Then again, Derin had never been ambitious. He seemed content to fill whatever role Dalton assigned him.

Devon, on the other hand, couldn't shake the restlessness deep in his soul. God made him for so much more than ranch work. He knew God's plan for his life.

Now, if he could just get Mami to stop dodging his request for his birth certificate. He needed it to apply for a passport so he could go on that mission to Guatemala before he started his teaching career next fall. Maybe she just forgot. Again.

Though, after asking six times, it sure felt like more than forgetting. Was there something Mami wasn't telling him?

Continue Devon's story in *Falling for a Smart Cowboy (Vargas Ranch Book 4)*.

# From the Author

---

Sometimes we get a picture in our mind of a person with a rough exterior or bad reputation, and we make assumptions about them. Derin defied my assumption as I wrote his character. I had already built him up in the earlier books in the series as a player. So, it was a challenge to think up life events strong enough to change his mind about the life he had been leading and turn him into a likeable character.

For characters like Derin, I am inspired by the dramatic stories I hear coming out of programs like Celebrate Recovery. Turning around is completely possible, especially when leaning on God. I hope that even if Derin wasn't your favorite Vargas, his turnaround inspires you.

It was a lot of fun writing the interaction between Derin and Madison, two totally different characters. I loved including the 101 questions and finding fun questions to help Derin and Madison get to know each other better. The idea came from a marriage seminar my husband and I attended a few years ago. So, it works great for any relationship.

Thanks for sharing the last few hours with me! Without you, it would not be nearly as fun to write stories.

Look for Devon's story in *Falling for a Smart Cowboy (Vargas Ranch Book 4)*. Another shocking family secret is revealed—one I've been waiting to share with you since the first word of the series.

*Karen Baney*

# About the Author

Karen Baney is passionate about writing stories full of flawed characters. She enjoys weaving together stories of second chances, redemption, and overcoming personal trials. As a transplant to Arizona, she loves researching the state's history and finding ways to seamlessly incorporate real history and real settings into her novels. In addition to writing and speaking, Karen works as a Software Development Manager for a Christian ministry.

Her faith plays an important role both in her life and in her writing. Karen and her husband, Jim, make their home in Gilbert, Arizona, with their two dogs, Bella and Daisy. Both Jim and Karen are active at Rock Point Church in Queen Creek, Arizona.

Discover faith-laced stories with characters who feel like lifelong friends.

Visit www.karenbaney.com to discover more historical romance series set in the American West. Follow Karen's writing journey and get behind-the-scenes glimpses of her research adventures on social media.

Facebook:  @AuthorKarenBaney
X:      @karen_baney
Instagram: @AuthorKarenBaney
BookBub:  Follow Karen Baney for new release alerts

# Books By Karen Baney

## Contemporary Romance

### Vargas Ranch Series:

Love is in the air at the Vargas Guest Ranch & Resort near Wickenburg, Arizona. Meet the Vargas family—five swoon-worthy brothers and their cousins who live by their family motto: "We do not deviate from the Lord's plan." These rugged cowboys run a successful working ranch and luxury resort while navigating the rollercoaster of finding true love.

Falling for a Fake Cowboy
Falling for a Real Cowboy
Honeymoon with a Real Cowboy
Falling for a Shy Cowboy
Falling for a Bossy Cowboy
Falling for a Smart Cowboy
Falling for a Humbug Cowboy
Falling for a Devoted Cowgirl
Falling for a Pregnant Cowgirl
Falling for a Cowboy's Legacy

### Steadfast Love Series:

The *Steadfast Love* series follows a close-knit group of friends as they navigate the beautiful mess of modern life in the Phoenix area—workplace drama, complicated families, and love that shows up when they least expect it. These contemporary romances blend emotional depth with authentic faith, reminding us that even when life unravels, God's love never does.

The Heart I Rescue (prequel)
The Air I Breathe

# Historical Western Romance

**Prescott Pioneers Series:**
Step back in time to the wild, untamed Arizona Territory where survival depends on grit, faith, and the courage to start over. Follow three pioneer families — the Andersons, Colters, and Larsons — as they risk everything for the promise of a new life in a land that demands both strength and hope.

A Dream Unfolding
A Heart Renewed
A Life Restored
A Hope Revealed
Hidden Prospects

**Desert Manna Series:**
Sometimes the most beautiful love stories bloom in the desert. Set in the growing frontier town of Prescott during the early 1870s, these tender romances follow women rebuilding their lives after heartbreak and the unexpected men who help them discover that second chances at love are worth the risk. Set in Prescott, Arizona between 1871 - 1873.

Beauty for Ashes
Joy for Mourning
Oaks of Justice

**Colter Sons Series:**
Power, legacy, and forbidden love collide in this sweeping family saga set in the Arizona Territory. The Colter ranch empire has weathered decades of frontier life, but now family secrets and buried betrayals threaten to destroy everything. As five brothers — and one resilient sister — navigate the treacherous waters of love, loss, and redemption, they

must decide what's worth fighting for. Set in Prescott and other locations within the Arizona Territory in 1887 - 1906.

The Reluctant Cattleman
The Roaming Adventurer
The Railroad Magnate
The Resourceful Stockman
The Restless Wrangler
The Resilient Bride

**<u>Larson Sisters Series</u>**
Meet the next generation! These delightful novellas follow the three daughters of Adam and Julia Larson from the *Prescott Pioneers Series* as they navigate love, courtship, and finding their own happily ever afters in territorial Arizona in 1886 – 1894.

In Love at Christmas
In Love with the Rancher
In Love with the Horse Trainer

# Desert Life Media

---

**Desert Life Media:** *There Is Life in The Desert*

## Entertainment-first Christian fiction set in the Southwest, featuring redemption, family, and faith

*Publishing clean, wholesome, and uplifting fiction since 2010*

---

desertlifemedia.com

www.ingramcontent.com/pod-product-compliance
Lightning Source LLC
Chambersburg PA
CBHW071909220626
47052CB00002B/269